Bashert:
A Ghostly Romance

by

Jonathan DeCoteau

Animus Nor Books

Paperback ISBN: 979-8-9885704-6-2
eBook ISBN: 979-8-9885704-7-9

For God, for family,
and for anyone who has loved

Table of Contents

Prologue

According to the Talmud, Rav Yehuda taught that 40 days before a male child is conceived, a voice from Heaven announces whose daughter he is going to marry.

In Yiddish, this perfect match is called "bashert," a word that to some signifies "soul mate," and to others, fate or destiny.

Part 1

CHAPTER I :

Aria in Soprano

∽ If it was Sunday, the roses were a ruby, the color of dawn spilled over their first meeting upon the shores. On Monday, the roses were a soft violet, the hue of settling night when Donovan and Aria first found each other's arms. Tuesday's flowers were a red as primal as their passion throughout their younger years. Wednesday's flowers were a delicate shade of pink, demure, vulnerable, like Aria, at Donovan's proposal of marriage. Thursday's flowers basked in the pure gold of their lasting camaraderie during their single year of married life. On Friday and Saturday, the roses were a white fire, like the roses that adorned Donovan's casket the day of their one-year wedding anniversary.

For every season of love, there were roses, and where there were roses, always there was Aria. For the past year, Burgundy Hill's youngest widow had kept to this same exacting ritual down to the most minute detail. Every day at precisely three o'clock the phone at the local Burgundy florist would ring, and one dozen long-stem roses, freshly cut, would be set aside, marked with an elegant "A." Precisely two hours later, an olive-skinned woman dressed, despite her professional appearance, in the elemental colors of ruby, violet, red, pink, or white, depending upon the day of her mourning, would pick them up, and without so much as a casual nod, walk out in silence, traveling the ritualistic path of her lover's demise.

Had the florists known that this Sunday would be the last they'd hear from their most faithful benefactress, perhaps they would have followed her to her altar, one tiny, nondescript slate marker among so many, upon which the roses were laid bare like some sacrifice to forgetful gods. Perhaps they would have asked the cause of so blatant a breach in her devotion, pleading for her to reconsider, to find her faith. But florists are not prophets, no more than slate stones are husbands or wives. And it was this final thought, or rather the repetition of it, across many a sleepless night, that brought Aria to the cemetery this barren, snow-drenched February day.

"It's not that I don't love you," she whispered like a high school kid breaking up for the first time. "It's just. . ."

Aria struggled with this latest blasphemy to the dead. She found it so hard to believe that underneath that stone, somewhere, laid the frail remains of the most definitive force she had known in her twenty-five years of life. There, among the crumbling clay, the haunting dun letters and simple, chiseled, dates, 1976-2000, lay the crooked smile that brought her to her knees, the shoulders, the chest, the body that was as much her as the flesh she walked around in.

There lay Donovan—her first, her only, husband.

Aria fished around her memories of this dead young man, certain that at least there he'd be an animate force, alive, profoundly so. But even the pictures she formed in her head were like tiny photographs caught on translucent film: still moments in the grayness of time, bound by clear edges, but in content, slightly blurred.

All that Aria knew was that, for each season of her life, there was one universal constant: the all-encompassing Donovan. The small, freckled little boy with a twisted smile who first taught her the secrets of nature in an unnatural world. The manic who sprouted from his baby fat to torture her with corny proclamations of infatuation one day only to rain curses upon her the next. The young man she swore she'd never marry, who, somehow, had stood across the church aisle anyway.

Even now, Donovan was just as animate as the distant memory that slumbered in a different kind of altar, one of the most solemn gray.

". . .It's just that I need the feel of fingers—I want to have a baby, to get on with life," Aria confessed, amazed that she could conjure the words.

Aria's raven ringlets swayed as she shot glances at the surrounding graves, concerned, perhaps, that even the dead might be eavesdropping on her confessional.

"For a year, this stone has been the only touch I've known. . . .I need to move...past you," she blurted quizzically, as if the slate marker were silent only because it needed further persuasion.

Aria looked down, her lashes wet with droplets forming like dew on a desiccated twig, her pale skin knit in contortions of pain, just like the day she first rejected Donovan by the seaside cliffs so many years ago. She knelt, embraced the stone as she might've embraced him. She kissed its coarse composition, its polished sepia, holding on and letting go in one eternal embrace.

"You'll always be my husband," she whispered, dropping the final flowers to the prim grave.

The thought of an elegant line, sufficiently sappy, perhaps something like *Death ends a life, but not a love,* seized her, but the weight of the moment was too much.

With unfeigned grace, Aria rose to her feet and wiped the earth of the grave from her colorless business suit. She picked up yesterday's white flowers, still ripe with the ambiance of the dead, and carried their remains to her silver Lincoln.

She smelled the flowers, took in the earth of them, and then offered them to the air.

Aria's reddening eyes did not dare to turn back. She simply turned the ignition and drove off from a small puddle of smoke. If her eyes averted at just that second in time, perhaps she'd have noticed how the white of her sacrificial flowers, lying in staid observance upon the lifeless marble, just then basked in the first drops of an ungodly red hue.

Aria's mother Bella always began her quest for grandchildren the same way: by bragging that her own child never cried as a baby.

The woman proclaimed that, even then, she was convinced that the girl was a blessing from above.

Whenever her mother joked about her complacent child, Aria kept quiet. How could she tell her mother that it was not her embrace, but that of someone, something primordial, of her own essence, that quieted her, some shared spirit deeper than even a mother's arms, than even shared blood?

How could she propose the insane truth that she knew to be as concrete, as real, as anything she'd ever loved about her mother? That it was in this woman's womb that she first felt the energy that she'd come to know as Donovan, this strange force who had not even been born until three months after his beloved?

Aria's mother had been a wonderful, if critical, woman. It was her womanly presence that helped shape Aria into the woman she'd become. But in Aria's only memory from her days as a baby, she could feel his hands, his presence, that of the primordial masculine, that of the divine, in the light that ravaged her eyes and welcomed her to the darkness of the world.

As in a creation myth of the grandest order, somehow, even then, the spirit of the man had wrapped his arms around her newborn flesh, held her, protecting her, breathing his essence into her as she first opened her eyes to the world.

His breaths became her first cries. She could feel him singing her way into the world, announcing her as a child of God whose time had come.

She could feel love, know love, through his presence, through only that presence.

Sure, Aria's mother loved to hint around for grandchildren by pointing out what a quiet baby Aria was. But how could Aria take the woman's words seriously when the very reason for grandchildren was no longer flesh, but dust and soil?

Chapter 2:

Orchestral Accompaniment

꙳ Rituals die slowly, and Aria knew that for the past year her daily life was little more than a ritual to attest to the questionable fact that she was still living.

The 1970 raised ranch had remained in her name. How she'd struggled to sell its dilapidated walls many a time, acting only now that the market was ridiculously high. It had been one year since her husband passed, and still the small, pearl gray house had become her cathedral, her last tangible connection to the man who was Donovan.

She fought to give it up, but the house, or rather the life it came to symbolize, fought back, so much so that Aria had let not even her mother frequent the house for fear of the chiding remarks she knew she'd hear.

Even today, she honored her late husband by falling into habit. Aria circled the old place. A brief tour of any of its rooms would more than validate Aria's mother's fears.

Aria smiled as she conducted herself on the sojourn of her former life. She walked just as she had done two years ago when her husband sent her on a rose hunt to locate all the gifts he had adorned their new house with.

Upon the chipped mahogany of the dining room table, an old cottage grove mission where Aria found the first of the roses, a year-old newspaper sat. It was the last that her husband ever read, still half-folded, untouched, in the exact spot Donovan's corporeal form occupied the last morning he ate his breakfast. The paper's crinkled presence, beginning, in the right light, to show the first signs of yellow, spoke openly of the dangers of the roadways, a herald of the death her husband would so soon realize.

Even smaller signs, like a pair of his black dress socks, carelessly lying at the foot of the table, spoke of the familiarity, of the comfort, that had been their married life. Each night Aria had reprimanded her husband for this laziest of habits, but now, after he was gone, the small, darned socks reminded her of the quirks of Donovan, of the other sides of his specious character.

Then there was the old ugly-as-sin grandfather clock, chiming away, irritatingly, at the hour, a prize that had been in his family for nearly one-hundred years. As Donovan's parents, long since estranged, would most likely never see the house again, Aria kept the odious-looking clock as a testament to her husband's heritage.

Aria went on endlessly, analyzing the chairs upon which her husband sat, the favorite coffee cup and coaster he'd used to start his mornings and evenings, even the abominable picture of Munch's *The Scream* that so entranced her husband he simply had to have it hanging just adjacent to the china cabinet he had custom-designed for her. This was the cabinet that boasted one of the first roses he left in her hunt of their new home.

A house is a shared legacy, and Aria could feel that legacy down to the last detail.

Aria, not without difficulty, left the china cabinet, giving it the slightest touch in parting. She headed down the hall that had the unique talent of magnifying any noise made within its confines to irritate any within a fifty-foot radius. How frequently she'd felt Donovan holding her in that hallway, letting its old wood sigh and groan for them as they failed to make it to the bedroom in time.

It was that touch she sought to recapture when she brushed past the wood each morning on her way to work, when she felt it, gently, now.

Even this day, one year after his death, the day she marked as the birth of her new, independent life, she treasured this hunt for the roses of memory. Aria reminded herself of where she found the last, most salient baby's breath Donovan had planted.

It was not in the living room, which still boasted Donovan's imprint, the echo of his flesh, upon an old barrister and an even older leather recliner. Even so, Aria could not help but take in what was left of his fragrance so long after he ceased coming home. She stood an amazing while at the foot of the stairs, before heading to the sanctuary that was so fundamental to her understanding of Donovan's being.

Two years ago, upon the house's purchase, it was in the bedroom that the rose hunt had ended. Aria saw it as a fitting end to her ceremony of remembrance as well. Not once, as she stood in the doorway of the old bedroom, could she forget that she had lost a husband. Everything, from the painting of the pink dahlias that was her present upon the anniversary of their first date to the cherry dresser drawer that had held his clothes, spoke of nothing but Donovan. But above all else, it was the bed that held the strongest reminder of his touch. Amazingly, though Aria never complained about their love life, she remembered the bed for a different reason. It was where, every night upon returning from work, the two nestled, simply holding one another, recovering from the long hours of work that separated them, a forced exile, all too long, imposed by the necessity of survival in a materialistic age. How often Aria embraced her pillow, let the covers swish over her in a fond remembrance of what had once been a husband's touch. The bed was where, born in separate skins, the two had merged. To Aria, they had been reborn, not separate, but one, in that bed. When they spent their first night there as a married couple, Aria had finally been able to call this strange house of creaks her home.

Two years ago, Aria found twenty-three roses, one for each year of her life, with one of an exotic, velvety gold, symbolic of their birth as a married couple.

As the night all too quickly whisked away the one-year anniversary of Donovan's death, Aria thought it only fitting to leave Donovan a rose before she shut the door and started packing the first of countless boxes.

In Jewish lore, there's a legend that when a man is born, an angel announces the woman who is to be his wife. The name is trumpeted through the heavens so that, when the time is right, the echoes of the angels will be heard by the hearts of those on earth.

Without ever having known the legend, Aria somehow heard the trumpets of Heaven when, as the littlest angel, she had met Donovan one Christmas when both were tiny babies. While Aria remembered next to nothing of her toddler years, she did remember seeing this most curious of creatures, another baby, for the first time. She had not even developed the cognitive skills to disassociate her own identity from that of the baby seated on a woman's lap next to her, which made her feeling at seeing the small male child all the more powerful.

While she hadn't the power of vocalization, Aria does remember that the baby, slightly younger than she, played with a tiny musical spelling toy his mother had given to him as their mothers talked. Over and over the notes poured, in the same blind repetition. Baby Aria, dressed in a pink Mrs. Claus outfit with a little Santa's cap, reached over the moment the highest note of the tiny toy wrung the air. Aria doesn't remember why, but that one note has always been associated with the one clear memory of her toddler years. For it was at that moment when her tiny baby fingers first reached over, recognizing not the name, but the power of the emotion, as she moved beyond her mother's caress, as she first touched another human being.

Aria hadn't an artistic aura, but the echo of noise against dead walls led her inside her own world from her youngest days on.

By the age of seven, she remembered playing with a doll she called Moppy, for its endlessly long hair, so much like her mother's, and another doll she called Crusher, *after the other baby's father, the man she dare not name. While she had never seen the massive hand strike down, she had heard it, numerous times in the echo of the other baby's cries. When she was a toddler, she'd scream, but the screams only fueled the fist, so she learned to grow quiet.*

Secretly, though, the infantile girl plotted, creating her own image of a hero she'd rescue, a romantic myth she'd feed countless times in her later life. Looking back on it, she was amazed how much the elfish frame, the striking jawbone, the mystical aqua eyes that stared endlessly into her own, were those of Donovan.

She hadn't met him since they were toddlers, and already she started drawing him, already a figure in the dollhouse was named after him.

Amazingly, even from the beginning, Donovan was a ghost, a boy whose flesh fit the picture, who could play any role, whether abuser or savior, Aria needed, and who, hauntingly, could vanish without a trace, ever present, ever absent, all at the same time.

CHAPTER 3:

Recitative

᠔ Aria watched Wallace rather crassly ticketing a few scapulars that would go to sale. The thought struck her: No one ever mistook Wallace for a savior, and chances are no one ever would.

To Aria, the man who arranged the giant garage sale of her former life was a savior of another order—not the passionate, all-encompassing entity she knew as Donovan, but an anonymous nondescript who had something better at the moment: an undeniable, and rather pragmatic, security.

Wallace's very features as he packed the last of Donovan's artifacts spoke of his devotion to the word. The tiny gut that nearly cleared the coffee table suggested the comforts of a sedentary life. The calculating pale hands that touched every last piece of Donovan's goods spoke of his unabashed resolve. The thin chest and neck they led up to, even the fat, placid face, spoke of normalcy as if it were a creed. As did the tiny twig-like eyebrows that fidgeted if any minute detail was out of order, and the eyes that were as black and unexciting as morning coffee without any milk.

While Wallace's luster may not have ignited the deeper chasms of the heart, the actuarial side of Aria liked his dogged predictability. A life insurance salesman, Wallace had never once engaged in anything more dangerous than eating his cereal without enough milk. And Aria postulated that Wallace had only done so because it would've been too precarious to his spotless record of untiring punctuality to run into a convenience store at an ungodly morning hour. What if he was two, say, even three, minutes late to work? The constitution of the man could not allow it. Even the slightest deviation in the carefully planned procedure he called life would throw the rest of the day out of order and the rest of the cosmos into disarray right along with it. Why not ask the sun to go dark or the earth to stop spinning? Either would have been an easier task.

While Aria may have found his job and mannerisms unwaveringly tedious and dull, she admired a man who truly liked his work and took enormous pride in its assured success. Wallace wasn't just successful; he was life insurance. To her and to himself. Aria thought it no stretch to say that Wallace took it as an axiom that having enough insurance was more important than drawing breath. It was more than a specialty. It was a borderline obsession and, to Aria, a bizarrely intriguing one. Aria had never before met a life insurance salesman so caught up in death. For such a pliable man, Wallace was undoubtedly The Grim Reaper of the soft sell. He could imagine at least one thousand ways in which turning a doorknob might prove fatal and nearly twenty-five-hundred ways in which everything in the common kitchen was more deadly than asbestos. And, though Wallace loved to prattle on about the poor, unsuspecting grandmother's danger of contracting salmonella poisoning and having her property summarily seized by the state, that was just a warmup for his forte. His real charm lay in car accidents, like the one that claimed the life of Aria's first husband. Wallace spoke so deftly about the delivery truck that plowed into Donovan's Datsun at an adjacent light that Aria could've sworn he was there. And how she loved it when he continually retold the story long after her socially acceptable period of discussing its most minute details had passed. Aria felt a genuine commiseration with the man, and that commiseration rather quickly passed for love.

While Donovan and Aria's first date took place by the ocean, and surpassed all of its wonder, Wallace took Aria to a jumbo shrimp place where his two-for-the-price-of-one coupon was still valid. But it was just this that Aria genuinely loved. While Donovan had offered and delivered the seven seas, Wallace never thought any larger than the most attainable of the tastiest morsels therein. His offering might've been smaller in scale and grandeur, but it was, just like the man, charming in its boyish sincerity. Here was Man made malleable: a man Aria could educate and care for. He had not the material to become anything like Donovan, and that wasn't necessary, would indeed be sacrilege to the shrine of her late husband's memory. This former mama's boy would never leave Aria. He was a walking life insurance policy, a man who would never have the audacity to simply up and die without completing the proper paperwork and seeing to its notarization.

Still, Aria's tolerant view of the man did not ensure his permanence to her. The tale of how Wallace could even touch, let alone ticket, any artifact her beloved Donovan had held in his corporeal days was indeed an odyssey in and of itself. Even now, his fingers moved all too gingerly along the last of the boxes, labeling each with minute care. It was as if those fingers assumed nothing that could go unproven mathematically, and with good reason. From the earliest days, Wallace knew that getting deeper into the house was no statistical certainty. The shrine of ordinary married life each room had become mandated that only a true disciple of Donovan's beauty be permitted therein. Wallace's very presence spoke against the eternal nature of love, or at least, against that of its corporeal side. This deeply upset the rhythm of grief that had, oddly, comforted Aria in Donovan's absence. And so, after their first date at the seafood eatery, and after their second date at the observatory, and after their third date at the theater, Wallace occupied the doorstep of the house and little more.

But Wallace, ever the calculator, determined that the 46.57 years of good married life he and Aria might enjoy could not be perpetually confined to a three-foot square inch slate doorstep. So he asked Aria to show him small vestiges of Donovan—at first an old watch or lamp given as a gift some years past. Then, once enough objects had been revealed, he'd work his way up in scale, gaining admittance to the lobby, where the few precious larger vestiges of a former life he had not seen remained, standing erect in stained mahogany.

Aria still stood in shock upon seeing Wallace run his finger across the frame of an old Munch post-impressionist era copy, but slowly, she permitted it, if cautiously. Wallace had earned the right as a mourner, as a man who dealt professionally in death.

Even now, watching hawk-like to see that the requisite care was shown, Aria thought back to how many nights she shared her true treasures, her memories of Donovan, with another man.

∽ "The table under that painting was a wedding gift," Aria confided, taking time to toil upon the last two words.

Wallace nodded in reverential silence.

Aria liked that quality about the man, that he knew when it was better not to speak at all. So few men did.

"I never knew until after the wedding that it originally had an ocher finish," Aria added, the hint of a smile taking the corners of her lips.

She made her way closer to Wallace, ran her fingers along the rich mahogany.

"He took time," Aria announced, "even when we were planning the wedding, to make sure that he refinished the table to make it my favorite color of all. He always did small things like that. I never knew everything he did. I never will."

On that day, Wallace nodded somberly, perhaps sensing that these little treasures were as sacrosanct to Aria as the holy frescoes adorning St. Peter's Basilica might be to the devout. Aria could see in his sparrow-like eyes that the man had contemplated moving his fingers over hers, in comfort, in solidarity against the coldness of an apathetic world. But something in him asked whether she'd understand the gesture or take it as a violation in this living chamber of the dead.

Aria, sensing the gesture, moved her hand from the table, allowing Wallace to catch the flesh of her fingers only in midair. Even then, she simply stared at this other man in her lobby, coping with the sheer reality of his presence.

At that moment, as in all moments of consequence, the phone rang.

Aria tilted her head, contemplating.

"I, I can get that if you like," Wallace proffered.

His vocal intonations rose and fell at each word.

Aria backed up, turned, made her way into the greater darkness of her abode. Wallace stood after her, advancing, then stopping, staring boyishly into the great beyond.

Just as quickly as she vanished, Aria returned, perplexed.

"It's a gentleman—it's for you," she said coolly.

In Aria's eyes was her accusation. Wallace could feel himself being weighed upon the scales of masculine virtue, could sense that those scales were tipping against him.

"I, I never gave anyone your number," he protested.

Aria kept her gaze fixed on Wallace's fidgeting. That was one quality about the man she never grew to love.

"The voice," Aria went on, "it sounded strange, but familiar. As soon as it spoke your name, well, the phone—it went dead."

Wallace stepped forward. Aria stepped back.

"I assure you, I'd never—" he stammered.

"Wallace," Aria whispered, looking at the man's patent leather loafers.

In his haste, Wallace had stepped over the threshold, uninvited. Wallace was now beyond the lobby, in the den. He shyly composed himself, but did not step back.

"Aria—you're alone here," he ventured. "Given that call, wouldn't it be more prudent if—"

Aria's eyes prohibited Wallace from even asking the question.

"Drive safely," Aria whispered, shepherding him back from the den.

Wallace nodded, mustering up something like empathy, before he collected his coat and sought out his only constant companion: the door.

Truth be told, the quiet that settled into the year of Aria's widowed life was not altogether foreign to her.

At times, from their youngest years, child Aria and child Donovan would just listen to the crashing of the tides. They were so lovely, so vast, the white crest-topped tides, so full of the romance of life. Neither of them spoke when the tides came crashing down. They just listened.

From the youngest days, child Aria would point out her dreams to the sea, which ranged by the day—everything from setting foot on the sun to starting a family. However silly such wavering dreams might have seemed, child Donovan never judged. He listened before sharing dreams that mirrored her own. They'd talk about what they might name their kids, about what a shared future might look like, as if it were out there, lost somewhere among the tides.

In fact, even as children, Aria and Donovan spoke so many times of their dreams that after a while, they didn't need to speak at all. They could just rest on the shore, in each other's arms, feeling each other breathe. Their breaths would lift and fall in unison, joining in with the stark salt of the air. Over the years, Aria and Donovan found a rhythm in their breathing, just as they'd found a rhythm in their dreams.

When the sun spilled its bloody pastels on unsuspecting clouds, the two spent the sunset as close as two human souls could possibly be, never uttering a word, saying everything and nothing all at once.

CHAPTER 4:

Polyphonic Ensemble

꧁ As the weeks passed, Aria was not the only one preparing to depart her home. In fact, the bloody light pulsing from Donovan's grave gained a life all its own. The light grew into a dense mercurial fog that seeped indiscriminately from the largest of tombs to the smallest of slate markers. The entire view of the cemetery more closely resembled that of a misty marsh from a gothic novel, where the gravestones were merely buoys in a great sea of festering maroon. This paste of color didn't just disperse with the night. The fog had tentacles that reached up and plucked out the sun, creating such a dismal account of death that even regular cemetery goers faltered in their devotion because the hue and its smell, that of putrefying blood, were so pronounced.

"The whole place is rotting," one local lawn care worker commented, packing up his equipment before he could even complete his task.

"I can't blame you for leaving," a frequent mourner replied. "I wouldn't be surprised if even the dead vacate the premises."

The light, the fog, the stench became so noticeable an article written up in *The Burgundy Herald* called for an immediate investigation of the area to see whether some rotting marsh weeds in the distant woods were the culprit. Other editorials from the same publication were hardly so scientific, speculating that the grave marker of a suspected slave had been overturned. The sensationalists argued that his ghost haunted a forgotten slave cemetery from New England's bloody past. The opposing editorial calmly pointed out that no such cemetery existed in records in all of Burgundy Hill, and that the nearest slave grave still known today was off in the Red Mountain area, inward from the coast.

Unfortunately for residents of the coastal community, as with many newspapers, the editorials hit closer to the truth than the news page. Something altogether unnatural was occurring in Burgundy Hill, in a piece of the world that was lost to the hands of spirits at play.

Donovan, or the spectral creature that once went by that human name, was awakening. The blood surrounding his grave, and now, nearly every marker, testified to a dominating emotion. That emotion was something that, in lesser shades of intensity, might be called, in the earthly world, rage. And it was not simply the graveyard's appearance that suffered. In fact, this parcel of eternity, this one spot of land that served as a portal between death and whatever came after, served as abode to countless phantoms and ghouls, from lost children searching out their parents among the ghostly fixtures of the past to ill-fated lovers constantly looking to be reunited with the love that was lost centuries ago. Deeper, still crawling past the tombs, were darker, outright malicious specters, ones whose lack of a clear form or a distinguishable face testified to the lost humanity they never truly had.

One might easily have presumed that Donovan would've fallen in with the lost lovers, eternally bemoaning his Aria, marching diligently among the graves. Yet, Donovan was not one to simply wallow in infinite despair. He had tasted the nectar of the gods, the love of that one soul most compatible to his own out of any to walk in the flesh at any age of the earth. And death had by no means taken away the eternal hunger for another taste. Instead, Aria's absence, and her lapsed devotion, ignited his envy, his envy his rage, and his rage his wrath upon all who crossed his path in this world or the next.

Most newly dead used the better part of eternity to evolve, to come into the fullness of life. Donovan, however, felt time more keenly in the next life than he had in the first, if for no other reason, because it was entirely unacceptable that Aria was not there, even for the most minute speck of eternity humans call life.

And so, feeding off of the energy and woe all around him, Donovan grew to dominate the other spirits. His fire blazed more deeply, seared more abundantly, until even the darkest of ghouls fled at the sign of his burning heart. Screeching, clawing, inhumanly, they opposed this uncrowned king of the phantom world, fighting his single-minded will until they too could take no more of the unending anguish he heaved upon them.

Though they fought to tear this new dissenting ghost to spectral pieces in this outer rim of darkness, of endless fire, away from the light, they soon fell to his darkness, became enslaved to his greater will. For their will only served his larger madness, and Donovan quickly became his own hellish sun. He dominated their less intense evils with his own, subjugating them until their knowledge and abilities became his, until his power grew well beyond that of his mortal days. It was in this way that Donovan mastered the use of spectral mists and fires, the conjuring of lightning and storms, the propensity for ghostly cries and telekinesis, and the power of mortal persuasion. An alchemist of the undead, Donovan searched over every form that came upon him for the answer to his dilemma: for a way to bring his love back to him. He took no interest in the eternal light waiting for all who pass, the light of judgment, of life evaluation, of ultimate, total acceptance, of total love. No, any light that was not Aria was to Donovan idolatry. And so, he became a light unto himself, extinguishing all others as he ate at them, joining them to his primordial fire.

All too quickly, Donovan's power spread infinitely. He practiced by terrifying mortal graveyard dwellers, spreading himself mist-like among the dead, choking the very weeds of life. Extending ever outward, he blotted out the sun, sending storm, lightning and fire upon the groundskeepers, upon all of Burgundy Hill. He brooded and dominated, calling out endlessly for his Aria, until his power grew sufficiently and he was ready to unleash himself on the mortal world.

Even from the earliest of days, part of Donovan's intrigue was that he'd never let Aria know where he was going. Such a mystery were his movements that years later Aria thought he might've up and died in part to keep his mystery alive.

Donovan was a ball of motion, a constant storm raging through tranquil horizons, and at the tender age of eight, nothing was more compelling to Aria than an unattainable object in motion, be it a bird or a boy. Aria could no more resist running after this fresh force of nature than a peal of thunder could resist shaking the stars.

And run she did. Down roads speckled with white sand. Past boardwalks burned crisp with the beauty of summer sun. Through the staggering sedimentary rocks aligning the Burgundy Hill shoreline. Up the chalky cliffs carved harshly against the scar of shore. Had Donovan jumped from the highest of those cliffs, into the arms of a surging opal sea, Aria would've jumped as well, just to see where this storm of a boy was going.

This day, though, it was Aria who became the storm. Up and around the cliffs she climbed, following the boy who gave her a pearl one day, not to bother with her the next, incurably curious as to what could possibly be more exciting than her reams of raven hair.

Apparently, the cliffs did not share the girl's sense of intrigue. Aria was just mastering a cleft on the edge of a chalky protrusion when her hand slipped and her body followed, down to a rock that marked the beginning of the low-lying cliffs.

Aria looked down at her knee and where there had been milky flesh warmed by sun, now there was a blot of blood welling, threatening to pour down, in a tiny rivulet, to the earth.

She looked up and cried, whether at the threat of her insides joining her outsides or at the loss of Donovan beyond the cliffs, her eight-year-old mind did not know.

But Donovan did.

At the second peal of misery Aria cast to the skies, he appeared, ducking and dodging the mightiest of the cliffs until he scooped Aria up and had her in his arms with the same security he had shown the mollusk two days earlier.

Though Aria could not articulate the sensation, she knew it: They both knew it. In that one simple gesture, man and woman touched, again, for the first time.

"Shhhhh," Donovan whispered gently, holding Aria all the more tightly the more she sobbed.

He brought her to the ocean, let its waves lap the blood away. Aria's left leg felt the tinge of pain, but the attention she received made even its sharp stab feel sweet as the noon breeze that caressed its waves. Her lips rose. A smile, achingly, formed.

Donovan was not deterred in his task. He bandaged the wound with a torn piece of his own shirt, then contemplated the odyssey home.

"Can you walk?" he asked diligently.

Aria put weight on her knee, but her flesh winced.

So Donovan carried her, hoisting her up until her tiny frame joined the sky, carrying her the quarter mile that to Aria might as well have been one-hundred miles. Periodically, he'd stop on the endless venture, brushing off his sweat, adjusting the bandage, just staring in disbelief at this deadliest of wounds.

Aria never recalled whether he gently deposited her at her doorstep, whether he kissed her wound with boyish charm, or whether he disappeared into the sun itself. All she remembered was that, for that moment, that one wound was everything, that, to Donovan, nothing was more important than the slightest cut on the knee of his beloved child.

And so, Aria smiled. And why not? For the small price of mortal blood, she had caught Donovan after all.

CHAPTER 5:

Strings

For weeks on end, the skies bled unnatural cloud formations that spat out only lightning and freezing rain. It was as if Donovan's tears and wrath mingled, painting themselves across the sky for all the world to see. In the small, coastal town, red skies usually bode welcome sailing, as the fishing industry knew no end, not even in February. Yet, it was where the masses of mist and cloud congregated above the cemetery, expanding ever outward, that was itself enough to deter even passing motorists on their way to the airport.

The papers, being what they were—anything but a source of news—capitalized on the weather, giving it top billing, even above local election debate coverage and questionable uses of municipal property taxes, favorites of the economically-minded denizens of the town. For the first time in Burgundy Hill's long and affluent history, tales of omens and predictions from mystics and mediums sat side-by-side with what usually passed as news. At a glance, the average consumer would be hard-pressed to tell *The Burgundy Herald* from *The Inquirer*, what with the interview from Mary Ellen Hill, a noted rich eccentric who claimed that the end of days were at hand. Less local visionaries were hardly more conservative, one going so far as to claim that the spirit of a mass murderer was on the loose in an article so similar to the latest horror reel that the film's producers actually threatened to sue the self-proclaimed visionary for copyright infringement.

It was in this inhospitable weather of the dead that Wallace found himself pulling closer to Aria's house in the only section of Burgundy Hill not to feel the pounding hail and see the ungodly mists that held the rest of the town at bay.

Anxious to manifest this to Aria, Wallace quickly parked his Porsche and met Aria at the door, breathless.

"I hate rain," Wallace cursed as he caught his breath and shook himself free of nature.

"It hasn't let up in days," Aria dutifully said, grabbing Wallace's coat.

"You mean weeks."

Wallace stood in the lobby. Aria handed him a dry kitchen towel and watched her fiancé cleanse himself.

How graceless the man was, so simple and deliberate in all of his movements. She turned back to dinner preparations.

"To hear the news talk about it—"

"To hell with the news. I just stopped over to see if you made it to work and back all right. If you were holding up in all these storms."

"I didn't go to work. I felt...sick."

"You sick?" Wallace asked, as much with the black light of his eyes as with his words. "You've never been sick a day in your life."

"Maybe it has something to do with the weather. I just called in and said I'd work from home."

Wallace stared vacantly, processing this latest anomaly. "If I didn't know you better, I'd say you were getting superstitious about the weather."

Aria nodded absently. "Not so much superstitious as tired. Incredibly tired. In part because of all this dreariness and all this incessant packing."

Aria let Wallace in, graciously guiding him to the Spartan kitchen table. Wallace sat in the cherry pine chair, the one next to Donovan's former throne. For a moment, he felt watched, unwelcome, like a usurper, as he observed Aria readying their plates in the kitchenette.

"Did you make an appointment?" he asked with strained politeness.

"It's not serious enough for a doctor's visit yet," Aria told him. "I just find myself sleeping a lot more. That's all."

"It's not right for you...living alone like this."

Aria served Wallace a T-bone steak that still looked somewhat bloody. Wallace helped himself to some red skin potatoes as Aria joined him at the table.

"I should move in," Wallace asserted, "at least until you finish moving out."

Aria's hand rose in supplication. Wallace's head jerked slightly.

"I'm going to be your husband," he argued, cutting his steak so as to avoid eying Aria.

"I'm fine, really. I'll only be here another week. Besides, I just...I don't want you to get whatever it is I have."

By now, Wallace recognized the stumbling of words as Aria's form of a lie.

"You don't want me here," he said, plainly, looking up.

Aria contemplated the man, the features that defined him—the unquiet brow that never quite settled, the stale, gray eyes that were always whirlwinds of frenetic motion. She should want him here; she should love him; how worthy he was of love, yet, how unlike her Donovan.

"Don't be ridiculous. I'm marrying you," was all Aria could muster after a prolonged stare.

Wallace's hands froze. Neither spoke. Without even taking a bite of his steak, Wallace rose.

"Wallace," Aria called out half-heartedly, rising out of obligation.

This time Wallace's pale hand rose, not in supplication, but in determination. "We're not going to have this argument now. You're too sick, and you have a veritable jungle of boxes here that I'm determined to help you load by week's end."

"But—"

"But nothing. Your mother's planning to stop by tomorrow to work out the final wedding details. You need to take it easy."

Aria examined the averted eyes, the descending arcs of the cheekbone, everything about Wallace's face, not without sympathy. Still, dramatic as her displays of affection had been with Donovan, Aria just couldn't see herself rushing after Wallace in consolation. While Donovan held much of the same restless energy, he made an art of masculinity, whereas Wallace made it a mere apprenticeship.

"If you're finished eating, go up and rest a bit," Wallace insisted, mechanically. "I should have the living room done in a few hours. I'll come up and see you before I go."

As Wallace labeled yet another box of old clothes *Salvation Army*, Aria stepped up, pecked his forehead. Aria could not help but notice how tremulously her lips indented the white skin that sat lifelessly upon the man she must love.

"I'll see you in a few hours then," she said in finality. She struggled to articulate her words with warmth and compassion, which made them sound that much colder.

Wallace nodded, lost to his packing.

Just then, Aria could've sworn she sensed something, someone, watching, almost as if there were a mystical eye buried somewhere in the advancing mists. She shook herself clear of the delusion, then started picking up after the dinner that never was.

The more Aria thought of it, the more indigenous storms were to her memories of Donovan. He had always been a tiny ball of thunder. It only made sense that he might be the media's ghoul painting his anger and hurt upon the sky.

He never asked for permission, never calmly or coolly said his case like Wallace, dependent upon the logic of it all. Donovan simply committed actions, his thoughts independent of all consequences.

Aria still remembers when the two found a sickly horseshoe crab washed in by the tides. How Aria cradled the small creature gently, not fearing its sting. Donovan, perhaps moved by this, also touched the crab, proposing that they nurse it together.

At first, Aria thought he'd simply propose the idea and then forget the next time some storm of activity engrossed him. But Donovan set out to build a small hut in the marshes, a tree house, only lower, where he, Aria, and all of nature could flee from the world and its laws.

How easily, how naturally, Aria played the role of mother with the crab, and Donovan the role of provider and protector.

When the sickly crab died, as all things ultimately do, Aria feared her home with Donovan would die too. She cried and wailed with all her childish might, whether at the loss of this creature unique in all the world, or at the feared loss of her new home, she couldn't say. She could recall, however, in great detail, how Donovan pressed his lips to her cheek, not as passionately as the kiss of the pubescent, but not weakly, either.

Though thunder and lightning heralded the death of this creature, Aria, oddly comforted by this gesture she neither knew nor understood, grew quiet. She still felt *the pulse of sea and storm, but of a different variety—she felt it inside her, an energy she treasured and dreaded all at once, as the one storm she knew would never die.*

CHAPTER 6:

Violin Partita

❧ Wallace sat in the cool velvet of his Dodge outside, watching to see that Aria's bedroom lights switched off, that she had relaxed and settled in safely enough. As he did so, he found himself haunted by years of coming in second in ladies' affections. It wasn't that Wallace never knew love; it was that love never knew what to make of him. Love was more like a quaint mistress of exotic breeding scandalously flirting with all the men at the party, hardly taking note of the bachelor standing mired in shadows off to the side. Wallace didn't know what to do with Love, and She didn't know what exactly to do with him. And so, as if by mutual consent, they left each other alone.

That solitude in itself was a tragedy, as Wallace was the personification of quiet, steady love, the kind that didn't fit into the romantic ideals fueled by Hollywood pictures, that would never win the hand of a debutante. That's not to say Wallace was altogether devoid of passion. Once, when Wallace was ten, he loved nearly as madly as Aria did her Donovan. The object of his affection was a sleek creature uninhibited by the social graces he knew he must at all costs obey. A young brunette, with shining skin and arresting olive eyes, she was at the center of every crowd while he lingered along the edge. She laughed boisterously while he merely chuckled. She reached out and openly grabbed hands while he kept away from the intimacy of touch. In her contrast, she looked all the more beautiful. She magnified the qualities Wallace so desperately wanted to possess, like a blinding light up against infinite blackness.

But Wallace never knew her. He dated her, briefly, when he calculated the best chance to take his risk, but there was always an aloofness, an aching distance. That, to Wallace, was the passion of love. And so, not so much by choice as by circumstance, Wallace outgrew ostentatious displays of affection. He became the quiet hand that held and held strongly, the nice, steady shoulder upon which so many women would cry. Most of his male friends laughed at the sight of Wallace with a woman. It seemed he made a better friend than lover, and numerous women placed him in that category naturally, never bothering to look beneath the surface at his greater passions. Granted, Wallace might never have been all romance and mania like his predecessor, but his passion was strong in its devotion, infinite in its unyielding support. Wallace was a man of feeling, but of another kind, so often mistaken for coldness. Many a night he wished he could've shared this with that brunette beauty of years past—and with Aria— but to Wallace the greatest love was unspoken love, that which proved itself by time and action. His was a love in which setting the alarm clock daily, setting out a towel for his lady, even taking out the trash without being asked, were demonstrations of the highest devotion. *I love you* wasn't so much in his arms or in his kiss as it was in the scraping of ice off the windshield or in scrubbing the tub. To Wallace, love was a clock of unrelenting precision, by which the days of life ought to be measured. It was a summation of its acts, not of its words or empty gestures.

Perhaps because of this philosophy, Wallace long ago accepted as fact that he'd never be the man that women fell for. He'd merely be the man to retrieve them after they fell. But did, he often wondered, his pragmatism make his love any less? So books and poems would never be written about his love of the ages, and gilded monuments would not be erected of Wallace in an eternal embrace with Aria. What was that but mindless devotion to an ideal that never existed in the first place? Wallace shook his head, reflecting on countless English classes he suffered through when he belonged in business school. How many Petrarchs ended up with their Lauras? How many sonneteers knew love outside of the sonnet form? Weren't they really making love to poetry itself? Would any such love have survived the mundane realities of life? What did they know of the woman of their affections divorced from the poem? Did not Pyramus and Thisbe, Hero and Leander, even Romeo and Juliet, have their discord? Was any love, whether legendary or real, ever free of conflict?

To Wallace, such idealizations weren't love. They were myth. Real love was real devotion, in the smallest of acts. No, no woman would swoon over Wallace, no troubadours would ever sing his praises. But how many of those men that women might swoon over would stay to make sure their beloved had settled peacefully into night? How many would, like Wallace, love so unconditionally, even when they were not held first in love? How many would sacrifice so much for a woman that Wallace knew, even now, was thinking of another?

⌒ Walking her nightly ritual around the shadowy objects that were heralds of Donovan's dying presence, Aria felt no comfort. She touched his old suits, even the silverware he'd last used, eying his breakfast spot as if it were the rarest of exhibits at a national museum. Still, Aria felt empty. Everything here was wrapped carefully, ready, after an eternally long year, to be placed in permanent storage. A twinge of pain ricocheted through Aria's trembling flesh. She felt herself cast in the role of betrayer, the role of denier, all this time after her first husband had passed away.

Aria fought, truly struggled, to confine her nightly ritual to three simple acts. But even as she brushed her teeth, flossed, then soaped and rinsed her face free of its makeup, she thought of how Donovan so frequently stood holding a towel for her to dry herself, of how Donovan was always there. Even in the earliest, most manic years of their courtship, Aria and Donovan often heard Aria's mother tell her so. Far from seeing their constant, aching need for each other's company as romantic, the older woman argued that it was unnatural, that two people who truly loved each other were self-actualized, whether together or apart. The old woman, in the few fleeting moments when she was actually away from work, often prattled on about what she meant, that the two shouldn't be so codependent on each other, that it was an unhealthy love. But Aria secretly thought her mother was jealous that she had never known so deep a love as her daughter. Only now, when Aria struggled to pack Donovan neatly away into the carefully labeled boxes of the past, did she begin to fathom what it was her mother meant those ten eternal years ago.

Aria headed towards the big queen-sized bed now devoid of the masculine clothing she often used to smell and snuggle before falling asleep. As her mother had warned, Aria felt as if she was only half a woman, despite being on the cusp of a new, vital marriage, of a second life. She threw the new purple covers, the ones Wallace had purchased for her from Target nearly six months ago, over her slight frame, then laid wide awake, fighting to think of her upcoming wedding day. Aria even smiled, an alchemist fighting to turn the small trickle of excitement she genuinely felt into a massive, swelling love. She tried to picture a small, but perfect, sun emerging from the steeple of a gold-christened church. She tried to picture the polished pews, the waiting altar.

It was only after Aria grew bored by Wallace's affordable reception plans, complete with his mother's hand-crafted cup holders—in short, only when she was dozing—that something like a jolt seized her. She sat up in bed, captivated by a familiar smell, that of the red flower she had so neatly displaced earlier in the day, burning. She removed the latent warmth of the covers, felt compelled to seek out the old grandfather clock that chimed away the settling hours. Stepping down unmistakably sterile stairs, numb to their collective chill, Aria witnessed a massive, ornamental burgundy glow swelling from the outside moon light. At first, Aria rubbed her weary eyes, certain she was caught between some night land dream and reality. As she approached, however, she could see a most peculiar apparition: a whole garden of supernatural roses of all varieties, from baby's breath to long stem yellow roses, appearing to wrap themselves around the clock, as if to stop it, then around the room, and all of its pasty wallpaper, reaching out, vine-like, towards her, from some phantom Garden of Eden.

Aria, secretly enjoying the dewy fragrance of one-thousand roses, reached out, saw a bloody rose light in fire and then crumble to ash at her touch. Oddly, she did not feel threatened by the cool fire that danced along her fingers before dying in the night. Aria understood the roses for what they were. He was there; he was calling. Her dead lover had returned from the other side of eternity, to reach out with a heavenly bouquet for his beloved. Donovan was there, in the smell, in the colors, in the fire, handing the assortment of flowers to the bridesmaid of his passing, a supernatural husband ready to make her a supernatural bride. Aria stood in his presence, so near, so far removed, choking slightly, before flinching, waking, and seeing nothing but cold shadows on colder wood. Aria stared minutely, then closed her eyes, sensing nothing but the distinctive smell, not of roses, but of him, of Donovan, that kept her standing in the frozen moonlight well into night's passing.

Aria remembered the last time she felt in Donovan's presence the same fearfully protective energy she felt last night.

She had finally managed to follow Donovan up the rocky steps and into the air blanketing the ocean. On one projecting cliff, the only one that could contain this boy of urgency, Aria felt like she was standing above the waters, actually walking on the sea, caught between Heaven and Earth. Standing on rock, air and sea all at once, she saw Donovan's small pale frame bend down, watched him cradling his knees, so miniscule against the massive horizon.

It was then, at the age of nine, that the principal reason for Donovan's perpetual unrest manifested itself. Aria could see the blood dripping from his bangs down to his knees.

I hate you, he screamed, again and again, frantically, spitefully, coolly, boyishly, when Aria, unannounced, stepped forward.

She did not need to steep her fingers in his blood to tell. The evidence soaked the sands all around her. This beautiful boy that held so much of her had been struck, severely. She knew that's why her mother introduced the two: Donovan's father was the abuser she once whispered about to Aria's own father, the one she prosecuted.

The revelation nearly toppled Aria, until she looked at Donovan once more. Aria remembered his humanity, the contradiction of it all, as this wounded creature softened, only to fight to escape her arms, when those arms first fell upon this wild beast of the marshes. Aria reacted as any small child might. She cried, wailed, unable to distance herself, even then, from the pain coursing through the young boy's body.

Not so much the tears, but the loud, violent echo of gnashing teeth, of anger made flesh, intrigued Donovan. He looked up, total shock glazed in his eyes as he recog-

nized the power of violence. Aria had never felt anything like it. She knew no word vast enough to encapsulate the frenzy of feeling. Aria was so desolate, so angry, so hopeless, so much in pain, frantic, unyielding, pulsing pain, all at once. She wailed at the injustice, at the violation, that Donovan felt in the face of an unjust world.

For a brief moment, Donovan stopped crying. Aria took over for him. She kicked the sand, turned over the smaller rocks, discarded them, and all Creation with them, to the tides below. In that magically manic moment, she became Donovan, and he her. It was then that Donovan first cradled her, first took her into himself, recognizing her, and she him, caught as they were, two small children in league against the violent tides of a world whose apathy knew no end.

CHAPTER 7

Bella (*Affretando*)

 Bella waltzed in the door without knocking, dusting off her fingers after handling the knob.

At the sight of this monstrous apparition, this mother of the bride-to-be, Aria knew her nightly battles would pale in comparison to her earthly ones.

Bella, for lack of anyone more qualified, was in charge of helping Aria shake off her emotional lethargy to undertake the monumental task of preparing for the wedding down to the last details. To call her help planning would be a misnomer, however, as Bella ordered first and thought second.

As Aria watched Bella hand Aria a coat and assume a seat, there was a deeper irony of which only a daughter could be aware: Bella hated weddings. And she was no fan of grooms either. In fact, had a man delivered the moon to Bella, she would've been critical of his impracticality. Indeed, Bella herself, bedecked in perpetually sable satin gowns that made an exhibit of her large, though sensuous, frame, made as much a hobby out of criticizing men as Wallace made out of calculating the odds of death in the most mundane of daily activities. It wasn't that she was a man-hater—no, she made a habit of marrying them one after another. It was just that she enjoyed breaking them much the way a lost love had once broken her. Given this charming pastime, no one would've guessed that Bella was Aria's mother. Their two natures, much like their physiques, could hardly be at greater odds. Unfortunately for both of them, nowhere was the war between daughter and mother more apparent than when planning a wedding.

It wasn't truly a material war, over cream-colored napkins versus those with just a hint of amber. No, underneath lay the greater divide. Where Aria saw romance, recklessness and excitement, Bella inevitably saw future despair—which she could determine down to the very week of its occurrence. Where Aria saw testosterone, Bella saw fresh masculine blood ready to be spilled. Where Aria saw men, Bella saw sniveling brutish swine just waiting to be slaughtered. This hardly made life easy when, with a single look, Bella could force a teenaged Aria's myriad boyfriends' estimates of their manhood to crumble. She knew precisely where to look and comment with unwavering disappointment—their biceps, their latest sports crises, their family's miniscule social standing, and when she felt particularly cruel, their acne.

Try though Aria might, Bella was a ball buster in sumptuous attire. Her brazen subtlety simply decimated the male sex, leaving no room for romance. Even as the master dame took her throne, bringing out a list of the latest seating arrangements, Aria feared and knew she was right to do so. Quite frankly, her mother belonged nowhere near anyone of the masculine persuasion and generally nowhere near people. Bella's forte was hardly what one might call socializing. It was stopping at mid-sentence and concentrating her glare on the most awkward and vulnerable feature of any woman's intended. *How's the roast*, she'd start, at one of her countless social gatherings, abruptly stopping, staring disbelievingly at a growing zit as if Everest itself were collapsing upon her very table. In a way, a falling Everest it always was—not in the form of any zit, but in the gigantic, and ultimately frail, egos of the countless men she emasculated.

As Bella prattled on about where the Astertons might sit, Aria knew: To unleash this machine upon an unsuspecting guest list seemed like taking that lucky something borrowed and reducing it to pieces before its patron's eyes. It wasn't that Aria didn't try. While Aria had seen, endured, even tolerated this judgment from her mother in the past, she fought it viciously when it came to her first wedding, when it came to Donovan. The young wild child Aria took too strong a liking to, in Bella's mind, was her perfect victim—full of every vulnerability, every insecurity, a man might have, masking it with an unrelenting temper that only revealed his thin skin. Long after Bella's interest in representing the abused child waned, her certainty that he was altogether inappropriate for her daughter grew. Donovan was a caged wolverine perpetually rallying to the attack, never realizing that, just by his having a reaction, the battle was already lost. That the daughter of two lawyers (one long dead, the other doing her best to end up the same way) might love such a creature was beyond comprehension to Bella. That her daughter might seek a union with him, unthinkable.

Hearing her mother's long-winded sermon about the virtues of having the two families mingle at adjacent tables, Aria knew that her mother would be especially obtrusive this time around. Her past misdemeanor wedding condemned her in her mother's eyes. This wedding was Bella's perceived triumph over earlier forces that ultimately proved well beyond her control. It was her chance to set the status quo right. From the moment Aria walked down the aisle with Donovan, who composed himself at least enough to talk to Bella, mother and daughter were eternally separated. Aria knew that this was the cost of her love, a price she all too willingly paid. Bella knew that Aria chose Donovan over her own mother, and was only too happy to take up a new hobby, endlessly critiquing her own daughter.

When Donovan abruptly died, and Aria fought to date again, it was this same incisiveness against the common rabble of men, against life and the world, in that precise order, that joined them once more. That's why Aria was so surprised when Bella had only the kindest of words to describe Wallace upon hearing of the proposal. For a brief moment, Bella almost seemed to be acting like a mother. It wasn't until months into their engagement that Aria could admit the reason why: Wallace was everything Aria was meant to marry. Donovan's death, awful as it may have sounded, was an answered prayer to Bella, who even one year later, had never mentioned his name.

Aria conceded a few seating arrangements, hoping this might settle this war of a wedding.

Then Bella opened her mouth and Aria woke to reality.

∾ Aria was surprised. How calm and how comfortable Bella was. Even when Aria brought up Donovan's name in a Cajun restaurant of her mother's choosing the very Saturday they went out to select the videographer.

"I just can't stop thinking about it," Aria said, looking over the woman's coldly made-up face for some remote sign of sympathy. "It's like he was right there. It's like he was trying to tell me something."

"Maybe he was. Maybe he was telling you that he understands," Bella indicated, concentrating on her martini.

"That's not what I felt. I know it sounds odd, but I felt like he was accusing, and then, in a way, proposing all over again."

Bella's pink lips slid, serpent-like, into a smile. Aria frowned.

"I'm sorry, dear. It's just that I had the same thoughts when your father died," Bella said.

The unflappable woman kept the words on her lips, until, even more than her martini, they were waiting to spill over.

Aria leaned closer. "I could sense his smell everywhere—you know, that combination of stress, sweat, and Old Spice."

Bella helped herself to Aria's olive and then added, "Your father's fragrance was all over the closets and the sofas. Then I got the house cleaned."

"I'm serious, Mother."

"Stop calling me that—I don't want people to think I'm old."

"He was there. Somehow, I sensed him."

For a rare moment, Bella's face looked matronly, if not maternal. "People die, Aria," she stressed between sips. "It's nice to think they live on, but to believe they really return as a mute patch of thistles?"

"Roses, Mother. Roses."

"Please, dear. You need a man. You've been living in that house alone for far too long."

"Only for another week," Aria said, sounding like some Greek chorus reciting an antistrophe.

Bella said nothing. Aria thought of how skillfully Bella averted all talk of anything serious, of how she always redirected the conversation until Aria's acceptable marriage was the focus.

"You lived by yourself for five years after Dad died," Aria pointed out in reply.

"That's because I didn't have some house-hunting wizard of a husband begging to live with me," Bella said. "But you have Wallace. And he has bought a house, dear, just for you."

Aria concentrated on a speck on the crystal glass, gazing as if some crystallomancy might magically teleport her away from her mother.

"I can't believe he told you about our personal affairs," Aria whispered in admission.

"He didn't have to," Bella said. "I know my own daughter."

Bella sipped her martini gingerly, watching her daughter until she was certain that today was not really about the video logs and photo albums she so longed to discuss.

"People say the first time down the aisle is the hardest," Bella added, trying her best to sound motherly. "People who say that have been fortunate enough to walk down the aisle only once. The second time down, especially after a long and loving first marriage, after the marriage you'd hope would be the one and only, is harder. I wondered if I was betraying your father's memory, if anyone would make as good a husband and friend. I had second-time jitters."

Aria nodded in dire commiseration.

"Then, dear," Bella said, unable to take more time away from her waiting martini, "I simply put on my wedding shoes and kept walking. Hell, I've made a career of it. And I haven't regretted it one bit—except for my third marriage, if that even counts."

"I can't do it," Aria whispered. "I'm not you."

Bella's eyes flashed in a cocktail of shock and anger.

"I know you loved Donovan, but does that mean that Wallace should lose out to—well, to a ghost?"

Aria shook her head. "That's cold."

"But it's true, dear—for a year now, and it's not like it's going to change anytime soon."

"But I don't know if I can love him the same way—"

"You're being impractical," Bella snapped back. "You lost a great love, but does that mean you should be the widow for the rest of your life?" Bella, sensing the argument was hardly in her favor, adds, in a matronly demeanor, "No two loves are the same. That doesn't mean one is love and the other isn't."

"I suppose."

Bella smirked. "Jaded. Check. Skeptical. Check. Minimal romance. Check. Welcome to the second wives' club, my dear."

Bella raised her glass, clanged it against Aria's untouched crystal.

Aria forced a smirk. As her mother rattled off all the possible appetizers, Aria could not help but think, *He was there. . .and he needs me.*

"I have just the thing to cheer you up," Bella insisted. "I know you already decided on a dress, but I've just found the perfect little place. . ."

Aria turned away from her mother's oncoming monologue.

She could feel that if she fell into this future, this life with Wallace, all events would be decided in exactly the same manner.

From the earliest of days, Aria and Bella were two forces of nature at odds with each other. If Bella said the sky was blue, Aria would point out the one white cloud that offset the color scheme.

Perhaps it's unsurprising that, from those early days on, Aria ran away from home, each time committed to the idea that all she needed was her makeshift home along the shores. At times, Aria grew so furious at her mother that she ran even farther, past the cliffs, towards the far marshes where even Donovan would not find her.

"I hate her," Aria would say, a storm unto herself. "When I have a kid, I'm never going to be so bossy or controlling. How dare she live my life for me!"

Aria would march around the marshes, preaching to a choir of crows, gulls, and finches. Most were uninterested and rather quickly flew off. Yet, whenever the world of nature tired of her, there was that one unstoppable force of nature that never did—Donovan. After marveling at the beauty of the flight of birds, Aria saw him standing there, his eyes asking gently if she was okay.

"I'm sorry," he'd start by saying. "I know you want to be alone."

"Then leave me alone!" Aria would shout.

"I can't," Donovan said, honestly enough. "Wherever you go, I'll always find you."

"Why?" Aria asked.

The question was too much for Aria—so full of angst. Why did her mother have to treat her this way? Why didn't her mother respect her will? Why did Donovan always have to be there? Why did it anger her so? Why, deep down, would she be even angrier if he didn't show? Why was nothing ever easy, least of all love?

Aria broke down, choking on the warmest of tears.

Intuitively, Donovan understood all these questions and more. He may not have had answers, but he did have the next best thing: a warm and unconditional embrace. After berating her young love, Aria always found herself at peace in his arms—in only his arms.

"I'm sorry," she'd say, mirroring his apology.

Donovan would just kiss the tears before wiping them away.

"Don't be," he said. "Let's just promise each other: However far away we may be from each other, we'll always find each other again, no matter what."

Aria kissed her assent.

How much all of her wanted to find Donovan—and his embrace—even now. How much all of her wanted to move forward with her life, with family and new love.

"Why was nothing ever easy, least of all love?" Aria found herself asking all these years later.

It was an answer Aria would never quite find. But she'd never trade the difficulty of that love for anything. Some fires burn too brightly to be ignored.

CHAPTER 8:

Strophe and Antistrophe

∾ Alone with her wedding dress, Aria was struck by how the simple pink lace contrasted so starkly with the elegant white silk she clothed herself in the first time. She marveled at how a dress reveals the woman, not the other way around. This dress, reminiscent of her second choice of attire from so many years ago, fit her almost too well: it was stylish, but conservative, décor with a touch of lace; it was long, but not a puddle of fabric at the floor—it looked like the dress a happy bride should wear; like her, it was wonderful at keeping up appearances.

The last time Aria contemplated a dress of this design, she was bubbly as could be, bouncing around the room, showing her dress carefully, but ecstatically, to all the bridesmaids she recruited from work. At such a moment Aria lamented never having sisters, but the sheer delight of being Mrs. Donovan Lee gave her an almost supernatural radiance. She was the glowing bride of twenty-five; no more was needed.

Now, Aria wanted to keep her latest choice secret—not so much to surprise anyone—just because she didn't want any to see that the original excitement, the unbridled love, was as illusive as the freshness of the dress. This time, the great god of love was money. Wallace gave Aria the numbers; she selected an affordable option. And just as Aria was economical in her selections, so she was in the commodity of the blushing bride. She'd sell her joy—but for one performance only.

Aria went to quickly dispose of the dress, still covered in plastic, neatly in a sacrosanct area of her closet reserved for her first wedding ensemble. At the moment the new special dress was about to hang, Aria felt a sudden urge, almost like a compulsion, to take the dress and try it on. She had been fitted in the shop. She also knew that removing the dress too far in advance of the actual wedding was not exactly the best idea. Still, she took the dress, modeled it against her petite frame, then proceeded to remove the dress, lace and all, from the plastic and carefully change into it. Aria couldn't quite say why. It's not like Bella was present, and Aria still felt a general apathy about the ceremonious day anyhow.

Moments later, though, she stood, a bride before the mirror, ready to take her march down the aisle. In a tiny corner of the glass, she could swear she saw a tiny, spectral groom standing as if waiting at the end of some supernatural corridor. Aria looked deeper into the glass, recognizing the fiery blue of the eyes. Aria stumbled back, only to feel something taking her hand, ready to pronounce vows. Aria jerked her hand free, only to hear—or more so, sense—the word, *Soon*, and her memory of Donovan's last words: *There shall be no till death do us part.* Upon the sensation, Aria fell back, watching her dress catch the closet door and tear as she lost consciousness.

⌒ Though it's hardly a common admission, some grooms blush brighter than their brides. It's just that grooms blush in a slightly different way: displays of bravado with a dash of sentimentality, pats on the back here, spurious jokes there—it's as if grooms are little boys going through a recital of saying goodbye to childhood and hello to life. Wallace was one such groom, and for him, love was in the details.

Wallace didn't just select any suit and pattern for his groomsmen and himself. He made a point of studying the elegant lace of Aria's dress, the touches of pink and snow white, and finding a suit, tie, and jacket that might complement his bride. For most men, this is a mundane task better run by the bride for confirmation. For Wallace, his wedding day was, undoubtedly, the most unpredictable (and therefore infinitely exciting to calculate) day of his life. It's not often heard of that men look forward to their wedding days nearly as much as women, but Wallace was one such man, and he intended to prove it to Aria with his attire.

There was just one variable he failed to consider as he placed the order with Grooms and Brides; he wasn't so sure his bride felt the same way. Wallace wanted to bask in the congratulations of others. When old men told him they envied his holding his bride for the first time, he desired nothing more than to beam with a pride greater than that he felt when he was voted claims analyst of the year by his colleagues. When young couples passed by during his lunch walks, sporting a baby in a stroller, Wallace wanted little more than to speak with them of how he might one day be a father—and then sell them on the necessity of life insurance. Wallace knew Aria brought out the best in him, as women so often bring out the potential of men, but he found it impossible to share this fully with a bride who was still at a funeral.

And so, Wallace tucked his catalog away, forgot about his suits for another day. In a gesture that would've perhaps shocked even Aria, Wallace cried himself to the point of exhaustion in the bathroom as he prepared for bed. It was only after Wallace waged this nightly war over the divided affections of the woman he loved when the phone rang and Bella gave him reason to cry anew.

❧ Pinks and ebonies swirled around Aria in a great violence of motion. For a moment, she felt as if she might be waking up to a world of undead forms, searching out the mystical light.

Then the light shattered, and she heard Wallace's glorious monotone.

Be careful with her, Aria heard Bella order an EMT.

"I'm fine," Aria protested, barely coherent enough to speak.

She looked over her body—elongated shoulders, short, stubby arms, petite, cream-colored hands and feet. All seemed to be in working order, even if cast in a pale hue. Aria fought to rise, until an EMT, a somber old man, held out his arms, cuing her to rest.

"I'm not going to the hospital in a ripped wedding dress," Aria argued.

"You sound like your mother," Wallace said, standing beside his eventual bride. "You take a serious fall and the first thing you think of when you wake is fashion."

"That's even more ridiculous than all this commotion," Bella complained. "Let my baby up."

Wallace stood blocking all the shapeless forms, until Aria lie in a tranquil black.

"What happened?" Aria managed to ask as the elderly EMT finally lifted her to her feet.

"We were hoping you could tell us. Do you remember anything?" the EMT asked before Wallace could.

"Just a feeling," Aria whispered. "I remember being watched. . . and assaulted."

"We'll contact the police," the EMT offered.

"No," Aria demanded, stretching out her weary arm in an effort to stop him. "Not that kind of assault. I mean there was this image in the mirror. It felt so powerful. Recognition, pain, a burning feeling—all assaulted me at one single second until I just gave out."

Wallace made a concerted effort to avert his eyes. Bella did likewise.

"I'm serious," Aria said. "I know what I saw."

"I believe you," the EMT confided. His old amber eyes radiated his concern. "It sounds like you blacked out. Heat, a feeling of suffocation—they're not uncommon. That's why you should get checked out by a doctor."

Aria nodded, none too approvingly.

"We've taken enough of your time," Wallace interjected. "Trust me—I'll bring her to the local doctor once she has a chance to rest. Clearly, this isn't the emergency we thought it was when Bella phoned you. For that I apologize."

The EMT's miserly, wrinkled face seemed stingy when it came to placing confidence in Wallace's words.

"At my age, I can't wrestle you into the van, ma'am. But I am noting for the records that you resisted going to the hospital against my recommendation."

Wallace was unmoved. "We know you have your job to do," he said. "But if you think you're ever going to get a slugger like Aria to go in her wedding gown, you haven't dealt with that many women."

"Don't be such a chauvinist. It's not becoming in a groom," Bella ordered. She turned her overly made-up eyes to the EMT. "But I'm here now anyway, sir. I can assure you that Aria is in the best of hands."

The EMT shook his graying bangs with emphasis and then headed out.

"Thank you for calling me," Wallace said to Bella. "But Aria seems okay now."

"Nonsense. I'm not leaving my baby in—"

"Mother," Aria said sharply. "I'm fine."

"We need some time," Wallace admitted, "to talk candidly."

"It'll only take a minute, Mother."

Bella eyed Wallace, almost adversarially. Then she sauntered off, lecturing the EMT on promptness until all that remained was Wallace, Aria, and the distance between them.

"I saw him," Aria whispered. "He was here."

Wallace made every effort to make sure Aria noticed the vacuum of belief forming around his eyes. "At least you didn't go into this in front of the EMT," he said in clear relief.

"I've never fainted before in my life," Aria argued.

"Humor me, then. Help me keep my word. Get changed. After you've rested, maybe have a bite to eat, we'll head to the walk-in."

"I don't want to go to the walk-in. Nothing's wrong with me. The only thing that's wrong is that my supposed husband doesn't believe me."

"Supposed husband?"

Aria grew quiet. Her olive eyes lost some of their light as Wallace stepped into the kitchen, asked Bella to place an order for Chinese food.

"I know he was here," Aria whispered.

Wallace returned just in time to catch the end of her sentence.

"Let's say that there really is a great beyond, and it was *him*," Wallace speculated, stressing the last word to make sure Aria heard him. "Answer me this,

Aria—why would he hurt you? This is your best, greatest love, isn't he? This Donovan? This precious name I'm supposed to never utter. If he is what you say he is, why wouldn't he be here to protect you?"

"Don't speak his name again," Aria whispered.

There was a definite undercurrent in her voice.

"Don't tell me what I can and can't say," Wallace argued, fighting to make eye contact. "Was it this Donovan who dealt with the EMT? Was it Donovan who saw that you were tended to? It's you who shouldn't speak his name to me."

Aria folded her arms, refusing to speak. A certain weakness emanated from the sweat on her skin. She looked like a chiseled statue collapsing.

"I'm sorry, Aria," Wallace prattled on, not without sincerity. "It's just—it's never just us. He's always there. His ghost has never left you."

Wallace shuffled, tried to assume a pensive pacing about the room. Aria still kept her eyes to herself.

"I thought I could live with that and yes, you were honest with me about it, but I'm not sure I can just keep quiet anymore. Not when it's hurting you. Sit down and ask yourself this, Aria. Ever since this ghost of yours began appearing, what good has come of it?"

An answer tiptoed over Aria's lips, but she refused to share this treasure of memory with an infidel like Wallace.

"So there's more you're not telling me," Wallace whispered after a great length.

The doorbell rang, the catalyst for an exit strategy that Wallace, no fool, capitalized on.

Aria, unfortunately, had an exit strategy of her own. She nearly fell over from the chair, struggling not to give way to unconsciousness. Bella and Wallace, upon sight of this dangling bride, dropped the delivery food to the floor.

~ A smirk flew to Aria's lips as she looked over at the counter and saw the windowsill draped in roses of all colors, all varieties. She felt too tired to rest, to simply fall into the peace of sleep, and so she devised a little game to wile away the hours. She squinted and timed herself to see how quickly she could read each arrangement's attendant card.

How many had sent flowers—Wallace, who still had not taken the thrift store label off of the vase; Bella, whose stylish baby breaths more than compensated for Wallace's frugality; a few of the girls from work, who had chipped in for a card which the other accountants, men mainly, had taken the time to all too tersely sign. Then there was a mystical set, an arrangement whose flowers grew over so many of the others, twinkling in myriad whites, golds, and reds, depending upon how the unique bouquet caught the light.

Aria felt mesmerized by them until she heard the familiar shuffling of Wallace's suede loafers, the pumping of her mother's designer stilettos.

"Another day at most," she heard a deeply accentuated voice declare. "We just want to run a blood test. Our earlier tests have turned up nothing."

"So at $30,000 a day for the emergency room, you still can't tell us what's wrong?" Bella complained. She was attempting, Aria imagined, to sound as rude as possible.

"Medicine's a science, not a form of magic," the doctor answered with all due snootiness. "When we get the results back from tomorrow's test, we'll call you."

Bella's eyes followed the doctor to the door, no doubt ready to point out the exit should he take but one misstep. Upon vanquishing their foe, the hazel eyes softened.

"I have every last detail of the wedding under control," Bella announced, a menacing smile wreaking havoc from her lips. "I hope you won't think it too much an intrusion, but I did go ahead and order Stilman Production Services."

"I didn't have time to compare videographers," Aria protested, futilely.

"Not to worry. I did. Stilman clearly offers the most reasonable package, and his film quality is quite professional."

"So it's decided, then," Aria huffed.

"You'll be lucky to get out of bed at all to walk the aisle," Bella consoled, seating herself next to her latest victim. "You don't need to be bothered with the tiny details of—"

"My wedding?"

Bella's cheeks flared to such a degree as to nearly set fire to her blush. She waited for the moment of insult to pass, then composed herself. "Don't be impertinent, dear," she insisted. "Why, at your age, if you don't make it down the aisle in a week, you may not—"

"Stop right there," Aria vented, "and ask yourself: Will I incur physical harm by completing this sentence?"

Aria sat up, utilizing the image of the damsel in distress straining herself to full advantage.

"I have no choice, Mother. It's not like I want to cancel the hall or the reception room. It's not like we're made of money. But it's not fair to Wallace if—"

"Not putting up much of a fight, are we?" Bella said, caustically. She let her eyes, narrowing like a cat's, imply her real point for her.

"It's not like I can walk down that aisle—not like this," Aria indicated.

"When I married for the second, even the third time—to that twit—you couldn't drag me away from that aisle, not with all the horses in the world."

"I will marry Wallace," Aria said with as much force as her weakened condition allowed.

"Then pull yourself out of bed and marry him."

Aria could hear a rustling in the hallway. Her eyes shot to her mother.

"Or tell him how you feel once and for all," Bella said with a smirk. "Actually, scratch that. I can hear him already. I sent him for some food for the three of us. It's not like I'd let us eat the food they serve here. It's beneath us."

At the sight of Wallace, his lanky arms placing some Chinese chicken on plates, Aria winced. She thought it curious that this would be her natural reaction: a wince.

"You brought that from home, didn't you?" Aria couldn't resist asking. "It's the leftovers from takeout, isn't it?"

Wallace mumbled about not letting food go to waste, then continued partitioning food out to Bella and Aria.

"Mother?" Aria asked. "Could you eat outside?"

Bella's strained countenance made her look like some pale human stop sign, an oracle painted in mascara warning her daughter, with one look, to avoid the path ahead.

"Mother?" Aria asked a second time. "Wallace and I have to talk. It's about the wedding."

Bella rose, took in the full shock of her dismissal, and shuffled warily to the door.

"Honey?" Aria began.

Wallace, in mid-chew, held up his index finger.

"I already called the hall."

Each time Aria reached over to discover some new life of the waters, he was there. It was wonderful to feel Donovan's aura next to hers, to feel the primal strength of his boyhood as she strolled the shallows, uncovering crayfish, starfish, sand dollars, and creations that defied a name.

"What's this?" she once asked, holding up a piece of coral from off a mollusk's back.

She listened more to the silent hum that was Donovan's boyish voice as he explained about the symbiotic nature of creatures of the sea, about how every organism had hundreds, if not thousands, of smaller creatures on it, about how they, like us, needed these creatures to survive.

Aria still remembers the thought that struck her: that this symbiosis was life itself, that it was only natural. The realization was so great, so wondrous and jarring all at once, that she ran along the beach, searching out the free air of the greater shores beyond.

And yet, not until her teen years did she become self-aware enough to question Donovan's obsessive closeness to her in the least. Even so, however many times she tortured her young love with other boys, other men, she knew this first and most basic of lessons to be true. She needed Donovan, and he needed her. They were simply symbiotic. It was simply nature, in its very essence.

Now, a year after Donovan's departure, as she set out the plates in honor of the anniversary of the house purchase that would never be celebrated, in honor of the first year of marriage that never was, Aria still felt his presence, still felt the security, the urgency, the symbiosis. Before it had been body to body; now, it was spirit to flesh.

As she laid out the lamb dinner she would've cooked, as she opened the champagne she had bought not six months before Donovan's death, in anticipation of the vainglory of the day, she could feel his presence there, smothering her. There was something not just sexual, but urgent, absolutely imperative, about this smothering, about the need she felt in him for his soul, his essence, to be not just a part of her, but within her, all around her, in a fusion not even intimacy could approximate.

And so, Aria lit the candle she would've lit for her love, looking upon it almost as a summons.

"Yes," she could feel herself articulating with the lighting of the candle, "yes, I will be yours. I am yours, always."

No sooner than she said this than the flame of the candle became a great roaring of supernatural fire, sweeping the whole of the kitchen until she could almost swear she saw a supernatural hand reaching from the fire to touch hers.

Breathing heavily, Aria collapsed in her chair, letting the preternatural flames consume her until she could take it no more, until she extinguished the smothering flame and left the house, driving aimlessly, fleeing as she had when she was a girl, searching for the freer waters of some other shore.

CHAPTER 9:

Crescendo

〜 A glorious path to the heavens adorned the small imitation frescoes of a modest St. Michael's Basilica at Burgundy Square. Aria stood for a great while, staring into the eyes of the parish's founding mother, a stern, coal-haired woman trapped in a photo from the past. Aria was caught in time herself, reflecting for a few moments on the repose of angelic faces beside a mural of Elijah, before she scribbled her dead husband's name in a journal of remembrance for the dead.

Ever since Donovan's passing—and even more so after having to deal with her mother and impending marriage—Aria had made a habit of attending weekly services, of giving her tithe to the church, if only to assure another Mass offered for her beloved. She always felt herself amazed by the widowlike devotion the attendants of Christ showered upon their Lord, of how often those attendees were the old and burdened walking the last of this life without the cherished soul that was to accompany them unto the grave. These people Aria could relate to; only time divided them as they gazed collectively upon the far greater divide death had erected.

Usually, Aria could count herself unnoticed as she took in the Mass, but today, as she placed down the pen by the journal and prepared her march to the solemn pews, a sound, at once human and sublime, stopped her.

"You only need to write his name but once, my dear," Father McDonald, a tall, sable-clothed Franciscan priest, asserted. "God will not forget it so quickly."

Father McDonald had been a missionary to Africa and Nepal who was rumored to have practiced ancient Christian rites of exorcism there. The hardness of that vocation still showed in the creaking legs, sloping back, and sagging cheekbones that defined his otherwise seraphic features.

"I need to save him, Father," Aria said, in a tone fully intending to establish distance.

"Only Christ can do that," Father McDonald reminded her.

"Yes, Father," Aria said dismissively.

Father McDonald was not so easily dismissed.

"My child," he implored, stepping forward.

The words were full not of condescension, but of honesty, even compassion. The man had been the parish priest and rector since Aria had drawn breath and, more importantly, it was he who baptized Aria, he who wed her to Donovan. It was he who said the funeral rites that would so prematurely signal the end of that earthly union. Just as he had said the binding words at the marriage of Aria's father to Bella, a woman he was once rumored to love. Indeed, Father McDonald was so old he'd earned the right to say the word *child* to even the most elderly of his parishioners.

"In my vocation," he continued, "you see a lot of tired, weary faces, a lot of supplicants, my dear. Many of those faces are resigned to the will of God. Yours is not. What is it?" The silence collected within the vacuum of his words. "It's the anniversary, isn't it? Of your marriage?"

"Of his death," Aria whispered back.

"Such a shame," the priest lamented, "that you can't remember one day without it also being the other."

"God saw to that," Aria announced coldly, staring into him.

The sallow light of her eyes was full of quiet confrontation.

"Men saw to that," Father McDonald said.

"Are you saying you don't believe in a divine plan that touches all, Father? That God has no accountability over the misfortunes of the world?"

"I'm saying I don't believe in men, at least, not in their ability to act with wisdom and compassion when stupidity and selfishness are so much easier. I've seen many great evils in my time, Aria, across every continent, but few match a drunk driver on the open road."

Aria's lips opened. Elocution almost came. Then, her lips closed. She took a few steps towards the pews.

"I'll see you at Mass, Father," she called back.

"He can't pass on," Father McDonald called after her, "unless you let him, my dear. He can't be at peace unless you are too."

Father McDonald gazed after Aria, sensing in the silence that surrounded her, an admission too great for words.

～ When Wallace placed the call, he could hardly believe the words that came from his mouth. After all, what explanation could there be that would ever suffice for pushing back the biggest event of his life? Burgundy Heights was by far the most refined and extravagant reception hall on the coast. They were lucky to reserve it even a year in advance.

"It's my bride. She's in the hospital, quite ill," Wallace heard himself saying.

The gentleman on the other end of the line expressed his condolences in a way that made Wallace realize the excuse only fooled himself.

"We have an opening in July," the man pressed forward.

A part of Wallace admired the man's sales instincts. "I'll have to talk it over with my bride," Wallace said. He offered profuse apologies for having inconvenienced the proprietor and his establishment.

"Of course at this late hour we can't grant a refund," the clerk noted.

"I understand. Thank you and goodbye," Wallace whispered, for once unconcerned with squandering capital.

If only that call were the end of his humiliation, he might've been okay. But the canceling of the reception hall was just the beginning. There were wedding registries to notify, colleagues, benefactors, and family that all had to be informed. When Wallace could simply say "She's in the hospital," it sounded urgent enough to elicit sympathy. But what could he say after the few days Aria spent there, after she checked out and returned to work? What could he say when the weeks passed and no new date was set?

Wallace shook his head as he hung up the phone. At least that mountain had been climbed. He attempted to sigh in relief, but the same tearing sensation took hold of his heart and he did his best to simply weather the feeling, too tired, too disappointed to cry. Instead, Wallace felt anger dominate his emotions, and began for the first time to contemplate whether his life would be better off without Aria after all. Since he was a child, it was his one, simple prayer request: bring me a bride to bide the days of my life with. Now, in his thirties, he was still alone, still without an intended, feeling old, isolated. As Wallace released the phone from his grip, it became more obvious that Aria could never be the bride of his prayers. But how he loved her. How he wished he could paint their life as a mural without Donovan perpetually haunting the canvas of their marriage. But wishes aren't good business. And neither is marrying another man's bride. Wallace nodded at the truth of this as he reached over for the paper and turned to check his stocks.

If she pulls anything else, he vowed to himself, *it's over. I'll just have to die alone.*

In the heavens, all things have a purpose, and to Donovan, that purpose rang out as Aria. She was sun, moon, stars, and seasons; even her laugh was like the wind jingling bells in winter. She had been there for every moment of his earthly life, his archetypal woman. Whenever Donovan saw any feminine beauty, he'd whisper her name. Whereas some saw her as downright homely, to Donovan her whole existence was a testament to the fact that there was still beauty in the world. While some may have seen her girlish brunette locks as less than ravishing, when Donovan stroked them, he felt infinite comfort. Some may have seen her frame as a bit too thin, lacking the voluptuousness of a fuller bodied woman. Donovan saw her as waiflike rather than bony. Some may have seen her sparrow-like eyes as restless pits of night, unattractive and even intrusive. Donovan remembered them as a gorgeous contrast to the snowflakes that adorned her hair like a laurel wreath when they'd play together, flinging snowballs at myriad passersby.

Donovan sensed, even knew, spiritually, that Aria would be even more beautiful once released from the bonds of her body. To him, beauty was no longer earthy, becoming less about the build, the eyes, the features she possessed, which were now like some fond recollection of childhood. Beauty became more about her aura, about that infinite expression of her eternal self that gravitated towards him as much as he did towards her. He noticed that most women considered less refined or outright ugly by the standards of men had, in fact, the most elegant and gorgeous auras of any in the world. But for Donovan, there was only one woman—all the rest were imposters, just as there was only one aura, and that aura was Aria.

For most souls, this realization of a boundless eternal beauty of which they were a part might've been a solace. For Donovan, what might've been comfort from God became a taunting from Creation. Unable to contain the supernatural need for union, his ghostly thoughts became his reality. Instead of seeing himself smothering this bride of the ages and extinguishing earthly life, he pictured himself gently holding her until she awoke in spirit. Instead of seeing himself as robbing those who got in his way of life, he saw all life as so eternal that in the grander schemes of fate, killing their earthly existence seemed but a minor intrusion upon their eternal selves.

Rather than console himself with memories of Aria, their entire relationship became one pressing, unified memory, a pulsing wound (with a scab ripped off) that needed immediate attention. Donovan's spirit raged, throbbing in a murderous red hue, until even the ghouls he dominated retreated from him in horror—until the balm for his soul's woes became abundantly clear. If he could not seduce Aria to the other side, he'd have no choice—for their own good, he'd have to take her there by force.

∽ The one activity Aria could engage in with minimal disruption was contemplating her wedding dress. She couldn't say why, really: she certainly was divided at best about the day it represented. But it was almost as if some supernatural force wanted her to wear that dress, wanted all to be mended, to be set right. Aria shook her head at the absurdity of the thought, only to hear Bella bellowing her way to the door.

"I'm here," Aria whispered, setting down some actuarial notes.

She unlocked the door, letting the bastion of a woman in.

"Is Wallace with you?" Bella asked, peeking around.

Aria was struck by her own response. She never even considered that Wallace belonged at her side on evenings after work.

"No," Aria confessed. "He had to work late tonight. Or so he said. He's been saying the same thing all week."

For a moment, Bella's face radiated in sympathy. "Don't worry, my dear," Bella said, clinging to some item under wraps. "I'll take care of everything."

"That's what I'm afraid of."

"Hush."

Clearly, the woman was too overwhelmed by the prize she held in her hands, for she could contain herself no more. She tore off the dark plastic to reveal the dress Aria fell in love with each time she saw it.

Aria gasped, then grabbed at the pink lace she so adored in the store. "I don't believe it," she said, in actual excitement. "You found another—"

"Yours was the only one of its kind they had left," Bella boasted. "They couldn't replace it, not on such short notice, but they did mend the tear. Look," she called out, exposing the lower folds of the dress. "I didn't want any daughter of mine walking the aisle in a ruined dress, but it's amazing—you can't even tell it tore!"

Aria circled with the dress a few times, touching the soft, yet grainy, silk. She then remembered, and grew still.

"Don't you like it?"

"I love it," she admitted, pecking her mother's cheek. "It's just the wedding. Wallace already called the hall."

"And I called them right back."

Aria nearly dropped the dress anew. "You what?"

"I couldn't let this day pass with only a week to go. They'd already rebooked it, so I offered them double the money."

"And they took the new deposit—already?"

"Burgundy Hill loves its money, dear. The date is set."

Aria's arms gave way. Bella had to step in and catch the white satin dress again.

"Careful, dear," Bella scolded. "I'm going to hold onto this dress for the week. I swear on my life I won't let anything touch it, not even you."

Abruptly, Aria felt her hands clinging to the dress.

"Dear," Bella said, making the word sound for all the world like a thinly veiled threat.

Try though she might, Aria simply couldn't loosen her grasp. She simply stared at her fingers, purple, pale, clinging.

"You'll rip it again," her mother argued.

"I want my dress. There's an awful lot of you and Wallace in this wedding, but this dress is mine."

Bella, clearly perturbed, let go of the dress.

"Weddings need planning, my dear. At the rate you're going, you'd think they plan themselves."

"My rate is fine by me. It's you who keeps pushing, who keeps prodding."

Aria took a seat, dress in tow.

"My dear, whatever's bothering you?" Bella asked, stroking Aria's back. "You'd think you're preparing for a funeral."

"Sometimes weddings and funerals are one and the same," Aria whispered.

"That's a fine sentiment for a bride-to-be."

"I can't do it, Mother. I can't go through with it."

"Why ever not?"

"I don't know. I really don't. There's part of me that wants nothing more and part of me that wants everything more."

"That's natural for a bride. It's just second wedding jitters. You may not remember, but you said the same before you were about to marry for the first time."

Aria peeked around at Bella. "I never said anything of the kind," she protested.

Bella smiled. "Of course you did," she argued right back. "Dear, if you and Wallace want to postpone, postpone. But I tell you I'm pushing you for your own good. Wallace is a good man, Aria, and he won't wait around forever. I want to die seeing you happily wed, with children every bit as wonderful as your career."

"You've made that clear many times, Mother."

"And it's the truth. Even so, Aria, I'd rather die than see you go through with this just to please me. I push because I love you, dear. And a mother can tell when her daughter loves a man. You do love Wallace, and hurting him would be an act you'd regret for the rest of your life. But if you thinking I push too hard, talk with Wallace in your own way. I'm sure if you do, you'll find your love for him again."

Aria kissed Bella's cheek.

"Get some rest, dear. I want you ready for the rehearsal."

"I'll try."

Bella headed for the door, but was anything but empty-handed.

"And Mother—"

"Yes, dear."

"The dress stays."

◞◠ Ironically, Donovan already knew he represented the answer to life's greatest mystery: love. One energy, one life force greater than all man's monuments that time would erase. Donovan's existence seemed a very testimony to this paradoxical reality; he knew it in the very essence of his nature. Yet, as he hovered around the meticulously clean Cape-style house Wallace bought for Aria's new life together with him, Donovan sensed that love was not the word he'd associate with this pragmatic little marionette.

How could Aria love such a creature? A plodding, accounting, little troll who knew the price of every last item in his Spartan home, but not the value of his own humanity?

In a way, Donovan sympathized with Wallace. The man, if he could be called such, had the good sense to love Aria in his own little way, but unlike the phantom that shadowed his afterthoughts, would never know the furor of true love.

Maybe one day his account would earn him a double platinum visa, but that would be as close as this little automaton might come to glimpsing the depths of unbridled passion. In normal circumstances, Donovan would hardly notice this pale imitation of life. But with Aria's fate hanging in balance, he knew he had to save her from the life of drudgery this Wallace creature would assuredly provide. The thought of possessing him, of using Wallace's body to hold Aria again, to feel her one more time, overwhelmed Donovan's ghostly senses. But he knew the end result: The passion he felt would threaten to consume and kill Wallace, and Donovan hardly wanted Wallace on the other side, messing up his plans for an eternal union with his wife.

Thus, Donovan's first interventions were small. Knowing that Wallace's world was one of assured order, he took a delight in taking out the smallest particle of his cosmos to watch the rest fall into disarray. Perhaps the car keys might go missing. Wallace's face would redden with a passion he never showed Aria as he fumbled around, hoping to grasp that tiny metallic object that might turn the ignition on his car. Afterwards, Donovan went through and reorganized the files in Wallace's briefcase, giving Wallace a rather creative weekend task of putting everything precisely the way it was. But when Donovan saw this odd little troll of a man preparing to sojourn with Aria for the weekend, his attacks grew more manic—and far more menacing. Any picture of Aria would see its glass smash mere minutes before she was to reach the residence. When Aria was reassured by her intended, preparing to show her trust with a kiss, Donovan became a great fume of smoke seen and smelled by Wallace only, who'd then cough until he'd have to turn away. Even in those moments, Donovan knew: This Wallace might prove trouble.

So Donovan's behavior grew more erratic as he practiced placing his ghostly fingers on Wallace himself, at first poking or pinching. The more he was ignored, the more the rage that came to define him took control, against his better nature. The spirit, perturbed at Wallace's endless obliviousness, became his darker thoughts. Donovan manifested violent swirls of red energy Wallace caught out the corner of his eye and just as quickly dismissed. On one notable night, the very week Aria broke off her flower tribute to his life, Donovan became enraged enough to cut at Wallace's hands and arms, albeit lightly, until Wallace had to wake in the night and spend his moments bathing his own hand in a mix of warm water and soap.

Watching the grim cleansing, even Donovan shocked himself with how easily violence could dominate his nature. He could remember nothing, not the cutting, not the spectral shrieks that accompanied Wallace as he washed himself, not drawing the blood that, in a few tiny drips, fell so freely over the porcelain of the sink below. In a moment of true pity, Donovan, watching the man in pain, vowed never to lay a hand on him again. Then Wallace spoke.

"So you do exist," Wallace said after bandaging his hand.

Donovan, more at the insolence of the tone than at the actual words, felt himself glowing in a spiritual fire.

"That's it? That's the best you can do?" Wallace asked, deliberately emphasizing his condescension. "You won't stop me. She's a good woman, and she deserves a husband. I love her," Wallace adds, with all the passion of a CPA on tax day, "and I'm taking care of her now. Not you!"

Bursts of fire shot across the room. Wallace, trembling, pretended to be the very portrait of composure as he stood statuesque by the bathroom door.

She's my wife, Donovan felt himself screaming, though the translation came only in reams of fire nearly burgeoning in the night.

"If it's a war you want, I'll send you back to the hell you came from," Wallace challenged, standing up against the fury of fire.

The fire magnified into rolling sulfur reams before knocking the mortal down and burning the very spot on his hand he had just bandaged with such meticulous care.

Shaking, Wallace removed the burning bandage, exposing a black mark made by the fire on the very cut he thought might heal in a day or two. This black mark smarted with the permanence of time etched into it.

She's mine, Donovan shrieked, before, in an ever-expanding fire, he exploded in reds and sables and disappeared.

The reaction on Wallace's face, the sagging lines that grew suddenly firm, the jaw that nearly opened, only to remain steadfastly closed, said it all. He had encountered the phantom, and he still could not believe.

The memory of touch is perhaps the longest lasting memory of all. Aria had remembered keen scents from her youth, like the beloved yellow fire rose Donovan gave her for the first kiss they shared in their earliest days. She remembered sounds, including those of wedding bells that still rung with resolve in her ear. But no sensation was greater than basic human touch, the once great sensation that linked all the other memories she still stored inside her capricious heart.

Lying alone, Aria can still relive the moment Donovan first touched her. Not kissed, but touched—in the way that a boy of age first touches a girl. The old abuser Donovan called a father had just lain into his boy with cutting fists, drawing blood all about the boy's temple. Aria could see blood elsewhere—on his shoulders, his legs, even under his fingernails—meaning that Donovan had indeed drawn blood too. When Donovan sought out the isolation of the long, winding bluffs, Aria, by now a master at spotting him, had sought him out instead.

"Go away," Donovan shrieked, as if trying to recreate the pain of flowing blood with his voice. "Just, please…" he whispered in defeat. "Just go."

Aria kept a careful distance, almost stalking the crazed boy. She neared. Donovan would hiss or cry out, cursing, crying. She'd near again, until the cursing, crying became less, until she could at last swoop in and touch the wounds.

Aria kissed the blood, sought out the shore. She ripped her dress, took its loose cotton, matted up the sea. Then she returned. Donovan, meanwhile, had begun stumbling off, fishing for other horizons, until she caught up with him, yelled at him to sit. Her words only propelled him on, until he stumbled and Aria cradled the angry beast into a sitting position. Then she treated each wound, softly, as Donovan fought the urge to stare at the exposed section of upper leg the torn fabric could no longer quite cover.

Sensing this, Aria kissed each wound anew. Donovan shuddered in joyous pain, flinched, but started kissing back. Aria held him, putting his head to her breasts. He sobbed, crying like a baby might, melting her with the warmth of his flesh. Aria simply held him, in what, for Aria, became the longest lasting memory of true intimacy she'd ever feel.

Basso Ostinato

⁓ Approaching her doorstep after weekly Mass, Aria heard a familiar wheeze wrapped in a lingering stench. Gazing up at the marble stairs, she stopped, swearing she almost saw Donovan's ruined face gazing upon her from the darkness. But no Jacob Marley staring from some haunted door knocker was this. Aria could still smell the hatred that putrefied the man she knew only as Donovan's very real biological father.

Aria could not help but stare after the man whose features so reminded her of her beloved. He had the same classical jaw from some sculpture of Roman antiquity, the same graceful lips that sloped into a surreptitious smile.

He stood about the same height as Donovan, 5'8", and had the same ferocity, the same wildness igniting his specious blue eyes. The aging man, lost to wrinkles and the stench of sour wine, was a living abomination to the shrine Donovan's legacy had become.

Aria stared, her eyes squinting ever so slightly, but she said nothing.

This man stared awhile, coldly, and then said: "I saw you at church today."

"I told you at the funeral to forget this address," Aria replied emphatically.

Her eyes traveled before her words did, sending a chill that rivaled any in the wintry air.

"I wouldn't come," the man said, half-drunkenly, "unless it was urgent, like whatever it was you were praying for."

"Is this one of your twelve steps?" Aria asked. "If so, I'd ask you to leave these steps out of your so-called recovery."

"I tried to stop you, but you'd gone. I called your work for weeks," the man accused.

The raspiness of his voice contained only vague hints of the voice that pounded his only son nearly as much as his fists did.

"They said—"

"What I told them to say," Aria added in finality. "Now spew out whatever it is that brought you here and then leave!"

"Can I come in? It's—rather urgent, rather—" the man whispered in a slur, looking around him as if his words had power over the earth.

"You showed Donovan the door and little else," Aria said in reply. "I'm not planning to do any more for you."

The old drunk withered, shaking his head painfully, scratching his hair as if trying to reconcile Aria's words with the bitter reality they manifested.

"You're right," he admitted. "I never should have been no man's father. From the day that boy came from my loins, he was cursed."

"Only by having a father who showed his love with his fists."

"Don't question my love for the boy," the embittered man proclaimed. His words, like most everything else about the man, carried the threat of violence. "It's not like I was all bad. Hell," he added, turning to leave, "I was here to help you. But if you don't want my help—"

"You'd be better help to me if you were dead."

The old man paused a second, then, staring Aria in the eye, lifted his sleeve. "You may get your wish soon enough," he said.

At first, Aria thought the old kook was merely putting morbid tattoos on display until she realized that these tattoos were made of human blood. She analyzed each—there were episodes of abuse sketched in the skin, followed by a cryptic date. One especially large tattoo showcased a swirling red mist consuming a man with a face not unlike the drunken ruin of a man standing before Aria.

"He knew I'd be coming, so he visited me first," the old drunk coughed out. "It was that monster who did this!"

"Any nut with a razor—"

"I'm not any nut. I'm his father," the man countered. He leaned in, adding, "And he's come back. He's come to finish me off."

Aria smirked coolly. "So you show up here, hoping if you're by me, you're protected."

"I show up for penance," the old man said, "before I die. You think you can stop him? You think any living man can?" The old man drank feverishly from a green bottle stained with the filth of his fingers. He winced as he took in his own words. "No one can save me now, girl," he said in resignation. "My fate's already here on my arm. I admit it: I'm helping you so the Lord may not send me to—to be tortured by other demons like him."

"Demons? The only demon—"

"He's not who you think he is—not anymore. I know what a stark raving idiot I am for saying this, but I tell you he's a damned, angry spirit, and he's not going to stop with me. My blood, my flesh—it's only a warm-up. For revenge. The one he's coming for is you."

Aria gulped, did her best to look unaffected.

"But you know that, don't you?" the old man speculated. "Why, if he's shown himself to me, I'm sure he's shown himself to you."

Aria turned her face.

"He has, hasn't he? And more. . ." The old man took another swig of some God-awful concoction, then stared long enough to conjure Aria's attendant eyes. "Get out of this house," the old man advised, "and out of this town. Get a priest. Get rid of him before he gets rid of you."

"You don't know a damn thing about him!"

"It's you who don't know what my boy's really like. You never had a full marriage with him, did you? You never really lived a long time with him—alone—did you?" The old drunk stumbled closer as he spoke, pressing home his point with his morose breath. "That fighting you heard on the shores—it wasn't always me hitting him, you know."

Aria slapped the old man across the face and then spat on the red mark her flesh had made.

The old drunk smiled capriciously. "I'm telling you there was a darker side to the man, something you never knew," he said. "If he's not stopped, he *will* kill. I tried to stop him when he was young, but I only made him angrier, worse. Hell, he took after me, all right, in all the wrong ways."

The old man's eyes looked drunkenly back across a sea of memories long dead.

"Don't want to believe me, fine," he added, stepping back. "But look into why his mother died. Go ahead and see why he thought of her as a traitor, the same way he thinks of you and that new fiancé of yours. Ask yourself some questions first. Then get a priest on him—while there's still time."

The old drunk took a few slovenly steps.

"Oh, and congratulations," he added, almost in mockery, "on the wedding. Had three myself. They were always nice."

Before Aria could hurl some choice curses down, the man walked away, eerily, towards the cemetery he was convinced he'd so soon join.

The old man's words still pelted at Aria's resolve days later as she researched on the Internet. Aria remembered the name, Regalia, of the largely absentee mother. Donovan had cried it out more than once when he suffered from his father's drunken rages, cradling himself, half-believing that had she lived, things might've been different. It felt impossible to Aria that so dear a name could be held in so low a regard. And, for once, the Internet held no answers.

Later that night, on microfiche, at the local library, Aria saw the clipping of the day the police had come to the small beach cottage Donovan avoided. A Sergeant T.M. Wilson openly suggested that the wounds were consistent with several blows by a blunt object, maybe even a fist. Not much of a mystery at that, it turned out. One Clive B. Asterton, poor son of a richer family, and Regalia's sometime lover, was arrested that night, but he was hardly the focus of the clipping. It was the first murder mystery in Burgundy Hill in nearly thirty years, and the reporters openly raved about the failed thespian's numerous affairs, speculating endlessly, feasting like literary vultures upon every ounce of blood, upon every inflicted wound.

Aria wondered why the old drunk would crow about this at all until she noticed a few peculiar features. First, in the subsequent articles of the year, there was no mention of Clive Asterton's sentencing, of his jail time. None of the articles mentioned alcohol in the least, and oddly, once released, this murderer was given full custody over his own son. Aria mused that the Asterton name must've still carried weight in the coastal community, maybe even over the press. She could find no further mention of the only murder in the town in her entire lifetime.

For a brief second, as the computer hummed, she asked, *Could that old fool be right?* This would be the defining moment, the one that ruined his life, that maybe even drove him to alcohol and abuse. *Why would he lie and seek me out only to lie again?*

The thought struck Aria that perhaps Donovan called out her name not in torture over her absence, but in guilt over what he might have done before karma came calling.

This is ridiculous, Aria thought. I shared a bed with Donovan. He could never kill. *I knew him, completely.*

Rushing from the library, Aria managed only to sit in the sedan, letting the gathering smoke of its exhaust symbolize her lingering mental fog. From her purse, she pulled out the one letter she never discarded, the first piece of bad poetry Donovan had ever sent to her. For all its clunkiness, its staid earnestness meant more to her than the very best of Yeats, whom Aria imagined Donovan ripped off, quite poorly, for his talk of Byzantium and gyres. As she sat, the last words of the unfinished poem filled her:

We don't belong to this age
You and I
Stuck half in Heaven, half in Hell
We belong to the stars,
To greater things,
To an age when people still believed

The Heavens danced for them,
Revealing their fortunes in the
Complex gyrations of the stars
Under some great gyre sweeping all of time
Collecting destiny
And painting it on the sky.
We belong to another world,
To a world not yet born,
Beyond the waves of time,
Where death cannot reach us,
Where love knows no end.
You don't belong.
I don't belong.
We belong.

Granted, Yeats hardly would've smiled down upon this young impresario, but at least Donovan knew the right poet to steal from. How could this boy, so fragile, be the brute his own father claimed him to be? Aria shook her long curls, kissed the poem, tucked it away, and put the car in drive.

An embrace said everything about a man. Aria had been held by other men before, of all shapes, of all varieties. Some embraces were too strong, either desperate or controlling, while the least attractive were limp, as if nervous or uncertain. Always, the embrace became the measure of the man.

Perhaps that was because Donovan's embrace had always been complete. It was as if every ounce of skin and bone knew exactly where to match up to Aria's own skin and bone, as if they were simply one body coming together, painfully, joyously, rather than two bodies seeking an awkward and equally impossible unity. The combination of confidence and vulnerability, of softness and absolute strength, held together by a touch of the sea on the hairs of the skin—that embrace belonged only to Donovan.

Still, an adventurer from her youth, Aria had explored the vast, unknown wilds of other men, and it was in this that she was cruelest to Donovan. She knew how socially inept he was, able to attract, ultimately to drive away, any girl who might flirt with him. Aria knew she had a more natural grace, an amiability that allowed her to connect, at least superficially, with any man she even remotely desired. And desire men Aria did. All kinds of men. In fact, the closer she got to Donovan, the farther away she drove him. How many afternoons would he leave the college hallways only to see her sharing a jacket and a kiss, with her latest triumph. It was a conquistador spirit she inherited from her mother, and one she could not, would not, deny. But always, no matter how deep the kiss or how passionate the embrace, the corner of Aria's eyes caught her exiled love.

The embrace, the feeling—it just wasn't the same.

Always, no matter how many dates she went on, no matter how many men's lips touched hers, there was a point Aria dare not cross, a point she knew was reserved for the boy she so adamantly alienated day by day.

The long nights Aria sat up by the grave, summoned by the first small flakes of winter, she knew that it was not memory, but feeling, that drove her back into the arms of the dead. Tracing her finger along Donovan's gravestone one last time, she knew that it was not memory, but feeling, that kept ghosts alive.

CHAPTER 11:

Aria In
Mezzo Soprano

꙳ For Aria, the world takes on a different complexion on a Monday. The riveting mysteries of the weekend have a way of dying as Aria crunched the numbers from the office where she wasted away her day searching out tax loopholes for a small business listed only as Tufia's Gate. According to the company profile, Divination, tarot, runes, necromancy, ghost hunting, magic—you name it, Tufia's specializes in it and all for an affordable price. Aria shook her head when she thought of how that affordable price was reached. Of all her clients, they were the most vocal, in this case about their request that they be granted some tax exemptions for a supposed church they were running and profiting from in a rundown basement.

This is not the life for me, Aria thought as she faced the prospect of forty more years of such absurd claims. While Aria actually enjoyed studying changes in tax law, she was a purist: She looked at each client of her company as someone she could greatly help by saving money that was legally theirs anyway. She didn't enjoy swindlers or others who sought creative interpretations of tax law so they could avoid paying their fair share.

Still, after she packed up for the day and drove over The Founders' Bridge, delayed by the inevitable traffic her own skills in road prophecy allowed her to predict, she couldn't help but think of this little shop on the edge of the marshes she and Donovan grew up on.

What if they could tell me? What if I could see it in her eyes when I walk in— that Donovan is still here, with me? Aria asked herself.

The thought was itself absurd. Just a run-through of the company's financial gains pointed to sheer quackery, to a steady stream of suckers who gladly bled their hard-earned wages for spiritual comfort from the other side of sanity. Aria smirked at her own naivete. How could she even consider stopping on her way home under the guise of a business question? What could Madame Tufia possibly know aside from how much Aria's bracelet signaled she might take her for? Still, the blissful irony of it was tempting: gaining admittance to a den of thieves with a lie, all the while gauging these very thieves and liars for truth she wouldn't have to pay a dime for.

Aria pulled off the exit ramp and headed downland to marshes covered in a revolting red fog separated by just a tinge of lightning. She told herself that she could feel Donovan's presence strengthening with the wafting of the winds, but quickly snapped out of her useless melodramatic mood. Aria, the business-woman, would have to handle this one, to keep her purse and her spirits under constant guard. In no way would she be victimized again; losing Donovan was brutal enough. The farther she drove, the more the flashing red neon sign of Tu-fia's Gate disquieted her. She half-expected to see pink flamingos decorating the lawn, perhaps as harbingers from the great landfill beyond. Instead, other than the absurdly large neon sign seated on a beat-up white shack, she saw scrawny seagulls sifting through trash on the lawn. This somehow seemed fitting as Aria parked her car and headed through the pounding rain to the nearest door.

"Yes, my daughter."

Aria searched the shadows until uncovering a woman of uncertain origins with an elocution reeking of phony patois.

"I've been waiting for the spirits to lead you to me today."

The woman stepped from the shadows in a revoltingly predatory manner so that Aria could see her; amazingly rotund, this oracle of the east side wore excessive jewelry on silky brown fingers and arms. Her eyes, though, were quite beautiful, hazel gems trapped in the fortress of flesh defining her face.

Aria looked at the woman, sought to hold her eyes, before revealing herself. The woman backpedaled, which usually happened only after Aria told people she was an accountant.

"I have a business question," Aria called out, stepping after the nimble giant of a woman. "I'm from Astor Accounting. I have a question on your church. I need to see it—and to see more records."

Madame Tufia stared deeply into Aria, squinting her eyes as if to reconcile Aria's words with divine providence.

"You need to see a holy man more than you need to see me," Madame Tufia replied. Her sagging lips took on an earnestness Aria had not seen before.

"Excuse me?"

"And to think, I never thought to see one in my lifetime."

"I fail to see—"

Madame Tufia advanced, taking Aria's chilled palm in her hand as if to see whether her skin was truly human. After releasing the delicate fingers to the air, the madam squinted around at Aria as if searching out her life story in her surrounding energy.

"They really do exist," she said after a careful examination of Aria's aura. "The *bashert*."

"The what?"

"An old legend my parents told me of," the woman began. "Come in. Sit down. I'll make tea."

The inside of the den danced in the light of a setting sun. Little specks of orange and silver illumined an entire amber brick wall of precious artifacts, from crystalline cats of olive complexion and authentic bracelet charms of all colors to books on astral projection and revenge spells that called out, tauntingly. Yet, it wasn't the lobby that attracted Aria's attention, so much as the spirit that seemed to settle in this place, a familiar, sweltering silence that weighed on Aria in its savage intensity.

"I don't drink tea," Aria said after a pause. She stiffened, though, and at Madame Tufia's urging took her appointed seat.

Surprisingly, the chocolate lavender of the sofa nearly burned her leg.

"You can feel it, can't you?" Madame Tufia asked. "His aura, all around you."

"Whose?" Aria asked, attempting to read her own psychic interpreter.

"The fated one, the one who was born with you. Donovan," the spiritual madam pronounced, as if from a trance. "To most people, the term *bashert* is a corruption. They think of it only as a soul mate, as someone appointed for their bliss. You know otherwise."

"Excuse me?"

"My father told us a legend once, that each soul is connected, a mirror of other souls. He said that at times two souls in particular radiate so vibrantly together that they become one soul, indistinguishable to the rest of Creation."

"Twin souls?"

Madame Tufia nodded, then continued adamantly: "Crudely put, yes. You see, forty days before a man's birth, the angels announce who his spouse will be. This wife is his fated one, his *bashert*, his other soul joined on earth for a particular purpose of divine majesty. These are powerful souls, destined to be lights to the world, unless. . ."

Aria asked for the completion of the sentence more with her motions than with her words, leaning her whole body towards the strange psychic.

"Unless they're ripped apart, unless something unplanned, unexpected happens in the course of human will. Then *fated* takes on a new meaning, my child. The one soul will seek out the other, won't leave it, won't be able to leave its aura behind. That's why, if you study the greater lovers of history, you'll see that so many of these twin souls die around the same time. Instead of the two growing as one, strengthening, the one smothers the other, killing it psychically."

Aria leaned back, her throat so dry she almost wished she had asked for that tea.

"If this soul is frustrated in its efforts to rejoin, why," Madame Tufia continues, "the negative parts of its energy grow, gaining power, until the union is forced. This happens rarely, maybe once in five hundred years. Your husband, he is one such soul. Death has transformed him into someone, something else. He will stop at nothing. He will even murder to facilitate the union."

"My husband's no murderer."

"He was not a murderer in life, no. You think that—that he may have killed his mother. It is not so."

Aria's legs jerked. She had to steady her body from falling from her chair. "How could you possibly know that?" she asked.

"He loved her and hated her. It was her that nearly killed him, leaving him alone with his father to take the brunt of all his rage. But this you know. Another question haunts you."

Aria eyed the dapper madam, sensing solace in her eyes. "Does my husband hate me too, for planning to remarry? Or does he love me?" she asked.

"He's in pain; it's not hatred. But he's—it's—not your husband, not anymore."

"Could a spiritual marriage, a marriage on the other side—"

"One spiritual kiss and this creature could suck away your life. He has power over you like no mortal has."

"But if I can stop his pain—"

Madame Tufia raised her fat fingers. "You're not listening," she insisted. "No soul driven to such excruciating love has ever been able to resist the temptation of union. Either one soul kills the other or the other, driven to despair, kills itself. This energy, this Donovan, it's around you, even now. It has subdued ghouls to its will, to help it kill you. You need a holy man. You must cast—"

"My Donovan would never—"

Madam Tufia's throat tightened. Her complexion grew especially pale.

Aria screamed, watching in pain as this force, this energy with which she joined, unleashed itself upon the madam.

"You have me," she cried to the energy glowing in red all around her. "You'll have me."

Seeing the madam drop to her knees, her body growing limp and purple, Aria backed up.

"Stop it or I'll marry him!" she screamed to the radiating fire.

Madam Tufia regained her breath, if ever so slightly.

"I'm so sorry," Aria whispered, fleeing the shop.

She did not cease in her running until she could feel the constriction of Donovan's rage around her own throat. As she stepped in the car, she could sense images of her mother, of her Wallace, all under the murderous hands of this raging spirit, who would not stop, not even at death.

There are some kisses from which a woman never recovers. Aria was blest, and cursed, to have received such a kiss.

The act itself was hardly extraordinary, more an awkward tweaking of the lips, a momentary touch.

But even then Aria sensed that a kiss is not made with the lips so much as with the heart. At ten, she knew that it's the feeling behind the act that makes for authenticity; the touch itself is only the icing, not the cake. And how Aria could taste Donovan, feel his heart beating, even before their skin touched. How she could feel his love struggling to take corporeal form, to communicate its profundity, its painful depths, in the scrunched-up lips, in the awkward flinches in the face of a ten-year-old boy.

How mechanical it was, and yet how spontaneous—both, taken by the sudden magic of the tides, craning their childlike necks, tilting and maneuvering their heads in strict adherence to the energy that bound them. Donovan gingerly leaned forward, missed, and Aria did the same, before, somehow, their lips met in the middle and Aria was never the same.

It wasn't simply boy and girl; it was the first time man and woman ever touched, all over again. It was every kiss that had come before, every stolen moment that would come after.

That's why Madame Tufia's words hardly astonished Aria. How much her relationship with Donovan was always like that, a bizarre dance of extremes, never quite meeting, until both collided, uniting, tearing apart.

CHAPTER 12:

Cello Suite

∽ Wallace had climbed these steps a thousand times, had dreamt of walking them a thousand times more. But now, as he stood alone on Aria's stoop, he felt as if he'd never truly left those stairs at all.

And yet, as the rain and storms of the supernatural came down upon him, Wallace felt that he needed to press on, that he simply needed to speak with her, even if he had to speak without words.

I haven't heard from you, he planned to begin. *Is everything all right?*

Perhaps Aria would look beyond the question, at the questioner. Perhaps she would see in Wallace's eyes that he loved her, too, that he needed her, wholly, that he could not perpetually share her with a ghost of a man.

How Wallace longed to express this, to let himself be seen lucidly. But somehow his love had become a mathematical computation, as if love equaled sincerity plus exertion squared. Alone and frightened after his ghostly attack, Wallace felt the instinctive need to be held by this woman he had for so long thought of largely as a suitable wife. He felt the need to simply find a way to express his love on a canvas upon which Aria could see, so clearly, all that was in him. Like most men, Wallace truly believed that if the woman of his affections simply knew who and what he was, completely, that she might love him. Perhaps if Aria knew that his love extended just as deeply as Donovan's, in its own way, perhaps if she knew that he was wounded and scared and needed her to call him, to check up on how things went, she might understand.

And so, Wallace stood. Waiting. Thinking of how he might tell her that even the first sight of her had filled him with an energy he never knew might exist.

That in his life of claims, excited as he was by fiscal acuity, a piece of him had died to the world, and that she had resurrected the best of him for all the world to see. But when the door opened, and Aria invited him in for dinner, Wallace could only imagine the words he wished to say, the man he wished to be.

"I thought you were going to call after work last night," he said in accusation.

He could sense, without seeing, the stiffness of Aria's shoulders, the flamboyant roll of the eyes, the arching of the back, the distance between love and reality, between words and emotion.

Standing in front of the mirror, preparing for bed, Aria beheld an eternal tunnel of light that stretched as far back into the mirror as Aria could see. She felt that, somewhere deep inside the endless refraction, was the essence of her beloved, burning in the fiery tunnel, fighting his way back to the earth. When Aria gazed long enough, she could almost swear she saw a rose of fire forming in the mirror, burning endlessly in the glass as Donovan struggled to take the form she most closely recognized. She could almost see the rosy image transforming into a torso, with arms of flame wrapping themselves around the Aria of the mirror until all was consumed. The rose took on all the colors of spectrum, even a supernatural array of hues Aria had never seen before, but sensed from this ghost of all seasons.

Aria stepped back as this form, this entity of a former name, stepped into the foreground of the mirror, endlessly advancing until it became the whole of the mirror itself. Deep within the swirling mass, Aria saw the face, the likeness of her husband. She saw a host of undead, unquiet spirits, heard a whole litany of cries, and even saw, in pictorial form, a brief glimpse into the ghoul's mind. Aria was to leave her body behind in a committal ceremony, in a marriage to the dead. Even though this one task seemed to consume the creature, Aria could see its rage manifested in the fire of its touch. Pictures of Donovan's father, of his visit upon Aria's steps, of Wallace, of his intimacy with Aria, of Bella fighting a smile upon hearing of Aria's latest betrothal—all these images surged like a pain as the fire grew into a blinding white. Aria could sense this rage controlling the other spirits of the fire, unleashing them in the supernatural mist that swallowed the town. She could even see the specter's desire to make Burgundy Hill a town of the dead, to destroy all that stood in its relentless path. Aria sensed anger, endless and unyielding, directed at a universe so unjust as to divide the two. She sensed pain, deep as the chasms of the sea, along with fear, vulnerability, even, all mixed in with the purity of what she'd call love.

"Give it time," she said to this eternal being. "I will wear an eternal wedding ring."

The monstrous entity, half-human, half-fire, swelled until it showed Aria walking a path of falling rose petals down a supernatural aisle. Still, she sensed, through this cry of love, a cry, equally powerful, of an insanity unyielding and unstoppable.

∽ Predictably, the pictures of the nameless dead man recovered, postmortem, from the shore, elicited the requisite chills from Aria.

She stared deeply into the sole color photo above the fold of *The Burgundy Herald*. Undoubtedly, the peak of the jaw, the arch of the eyebrow, even the shape of the contorted face, resembled the man who had stood on her stoop, terrifying her, not three days ago—the man who looked so much like the ruins of her first husband. Aria forced her eyes to follow the cold, black letters that all pointed to the most morose quality of the photo: the reddened flesh that the man had exposed to Aria, that he frantically claimed signaled his fate.

Aria analyzed the picture, but the widow in her revisited another picture, so much like it, only a year ago. The chill of the dead still firmly perched on her shoulders, Aria relived seeing the same image on the same newspaper the day after her husband died in his hospital bed.

Flower Truck Kills Valentine Shopper, the ironic headline had read. How cruel headlines can be, even more so when they're true. Aria didn't know what to think of the event, particularly when the headline of the latest photo read *Mystery Truck Kills Pedestrian*. It all sounded so eerily familiar. According to the report, a truck had hit a homeless man near Ocean Avenue, knocking him into the brush just before the shore. It was a quick, ruthlessly efficient form of death. The man had simply been struck and died in a pool of his blood.

Oddly, the headline wasn't even the most ominous on the page. *Missing Teen Couple Found Dead* and *Police Suspect Valentine Serial Killer* shared equal, if not greater, space. The eeriest headline, staring back at her from well beneath the fold, speculated: *Eyewitness Account of Valentine's Day Ghost.* Aria knew the headline referred not to a spirit as to this alleged killer, whose ability to disappear so quickly, undetected, along with his choice of victims, had earned him the name. Still, the drawing printed in the paper bore shadowy similarities to the face, to the cheekbones and eyes, of her own lost love.

Aria flung the paper into the trash. She missed, watching as the paper crumpled up into a sad collection of pulp, gathering in the dust that congregated along the wooden edge of the floor.

⌒ "He's dead," Aria whispered, struggling to convince herself.

She composed herself enough to grab her jacket, to go for a walk near the shore. As the mortuaries of cattails and dead shallow water weeds sat frozen in decay, Aria couldn't help but think of how ironic it was. This decaying sanctuary was the one place where she remembered her transformation from girl to woman. How natural it all felt, just before Donovan's father caught them, the touch of her lover, reclaiming her after all her exploits with the town boys, reminding her of what true intimacy felt like. With him, sex was not an act, but a ritual, as holy, as wild, as full of spirit as any religious relic of a forgotten age. To Aria, Donovan was the corporeal form of passion. When Donovan's father found them, ridiculing Donovan for his lechery, that man became the corporeal form of hate.

Aria shook herself free of memory and looked at the chilled canvas before her. Now, there was no sudden frenzy of energy between her legs. There was simply coldness looking out from the dying face of nature. Still, beside all the ferns and sands, Aria felt a presence, a spirit of the place that had already come to life. The wind kicked up, the weeds and ferns beat in time, as Aria felt the reddened particles of sand where Donovan's father fell flying at her in ruthless abandon. For a sheer moment, she saw the old man's death, the truck hitting, the blood flying, even sensed the excruciating moment of shock and pain before the great collapse.

"Leave me alone!" she screamed to the restless ferns.

The ferns, as if in reply, ceased in their dancing, as did the weeds, the waves, and the sands, just long enough for Aria to sense a figure looking out from the sands, a strange face buried in darkness.

Donovan could never do this. The Donovan she knew was nothing but a sensitive soul thrust into the most insensitive of worlds. He respected life, respected Aria, and was perhaps the first man to truly do so.

So immediate was the power of memory that Aria could still surround herself with her twelve-year-old world, could still remember the birthday her father, away on legal affairs, forgot. How she had waited for that call, pretending to be nonchalant, wondering what great gift her father would devise for her. It was nearly night before Aria realized that not just her father, but even her meticulous mother, had forgotten her birthday. She struggled to come to terms with this new isolation puberty seemed to bring to the situation. She sat along the beach, her feet cradling the sand of the washing tides, staring out into the endless expanse of ocean, the only sight large enough to quantify her grief. Her parents didn't care. Mark, her first boyfriend after Donovan, had dumped her weeks ago and naturally hadn't even sent a card. Every heartbeat pounded out a truth as cold as the tides: Aria couldn't be more alone than at the age of twelve.

It was then that Donovan, that this supposed patricidal ghoul, came to her. He had a card, one he drew, and a gift of pearls he'd collected—perhaps even stole, from clams harvested on private waters for just this reason. He didn't say a word, didn't have to. He instinctively handed both card and necklace to Aria and then sat with her, watching the tides. Donovan's mere presence was her gift, only a few months after she'd arrogantly claimed she'd outgrown him, after she'd so selfishly feasted on the attention of other newly pubescent boys. What a gift he was—more faithful, more omnipresent, than any creature she'd ever come to know.

When Aria did finally feel like speaking, several minutes later, when she finally revealed the embarrassing truth to him, it was Donovan who formed her a cake from the wet sands, who compelled her by charm into helping him put on the precise number of sandy candles in the last embers of daylight. After compelling her to make a wish, Donovan simply sung "Happy Birthday," cradling her as they stared at the infinite ocean. He just sung and held her, in those simple gestures changing her worst birthday into the greatest she'd ever know.

This selfless boy, who forgave Aria her many sins before she even finished committing them, who forgave her similar sins that in her lust she would most definitely commit, this embodiment of truly unconditional love, was a murderer? Aria shook her head. To admit that the monster and the man could co-exist would be the same as to say that her memories, that all that was left of her, were nothing but lies washed thin by the tides of time.

CHAPTER 13:

Choral Rising

Reports circulated the news; according to the mayor himself, the affluent coastal community of Burgundy Hill had become a ghost town. What made the story particularly salient was that Mayor Chelsea had, in a brazen act of political suicide, taken to drafting paperwork declaring a state of emergency and asking for state-funded help. The cause: a supernatural disaster. Reporters circulated, more numerous than the ghosts upon which they reported. Press conferences ceaselessly focused on the frustrated mayor as he took the podium, his graying hairs tinged in translucent sweat, saying that local scientists could find no definite natural explanation for the red fog or for the numerous sightings it seemed to agitate. By the end of the next week, it became lucid: Burgundy Hill would live in history as the site of perhaps the most peculiar case of mass hysteria in the western world.

Already the pundits were taking to the vacuous outlets of cable television, along with mystics and psychic mediums of various degrees of incredulity. Suddenly, every spiritual medium was an expert on Burgundy Hill, its inhabitants, and its spectral Valentine's Day killer, who, according to one report, was the soul of Black Beard himself returned from the sea. Faces permeated the news; "unaltered" photographs descended upon the airwaves, capturing myriad phantom infestations. Internet sites broadened the supposed hoax, manipulating countless photos and devising pseudo-messages of Apocalypse from the other side. Sightings like Aria's that night at the beach were miniscule in comparison, as, in the most famous Internet photos, entire legions of spirits were shown defacing the street walkways.

In all of this, Bella was undeterred. The mistress of failed marriages simply turned off the television, labeling it all rubbish anyway, and turned towards the one event no supernatural doomsday could ruin: her only daughter's wedding. When Aria drove through the dense fog, locked up her car, and headed in, her mother was the one ghoul she could not exorcise.

"I have fantastic news, dear," Bella declared with genuine maternal glee. "The hall is still ours."

"Mother!"

Aria sat, started sifting through the mail.

"I couldn't see my only daughter postpone her wedding on account of a little faint."

"A little faint?"

"And the most wonderful part is that Wallace agrees!"

"Does he?" Aria snorted her disgust. "And just where is Wallace?"

"He's coming to tell you himself, but I just couldn't wait. You see, that's the best news of all, dear," Bella said, pausing to add the requisite drama to the moment. "Wallace has spoken with the realtor today."

Aria's face became a reddish haze. Her eyes ignited like old flint taken once too often by the flame.

"The house has sold for just over $400,000!" Bella blurted out.

"$400,000?" The bills slipped from Aria's fingers, careening to the floor. "But who in their right mind—"

"Who, yes, that's a relevant question. In their right mind—well, no, they're not. It seems the ghost scare has actually driven up the property values. Remember that show *Spirit Seekers*."

"Oh, no."

"Oh, yes! They're basing their entire next season on Burgundy Hill, and they just happened to be seeking prime real estate to set up shop in."

Bella grasped her daughter's shoulders in a moment of unfeigned excitement.

"How long do we have before. . ." Aria paused, gulping.

"I told them you'd be out by next Saturday!"

"By my wedding day!" Aria said, freeing herself of her mother's touch.

She paced, then took to the nearest sofa.

"It's perfect, dear. Really," Bella said, sitting so close to Aria she was almost atop her. "By the time you and Wallace return from your honeymoon, I'll have your new house all set up!"

"Get out!" Aria screamed.

She jumped up, sought to move, to communicate the enormity of emotion, only to remain paralyzed, empty, and impotent.

Suffusion settled all over Bella's cheeks. "I would think—"

"That's the trouble, Mother. You never stop to think! Had you—"

"What's all this about?" a voice called from the door.

"Your bride's in need of some cheer," Bella suggested, sounding so sprightly it came across as catty.

"Has she heard the news?"

"Heard, yes. Listened—apparently, not."

Wallace's face emerged from a wisp of fog that followed along his coattails. His countenance looked especially constricted, as if some wayward event had so unnerved the man that his skin jumped off and needed to be refitted to his face.

"What's wrong?" Aria asked immediately, sitting once more.

"The house?" Bella asked before Aria could even get out her words.

Wallace shook his head. "It's nothing. I just thought you'd be pleased is all," he said flatly.

"Any sensible woman would be," Bella muttered.

"I am," Aria said with forced conviction. "It's just—couldn't you have waited until after the wedding day?"

"I'll need every day of your week in Bermuda to—"

"There's something you're not telling me," Aria interrupted, prodding Wallace with her eyes.

"It's just the house. It sold—well, higher than anticipated. The realtor was able to drum it up to $425,000 paid by a last-minute buyer."

Bella squealed in feminine delight, embracing Wallace as if he were some conquistador of capitalism returned from battle. Aria just stared deeper into the man, questioning.

∽ Colors never before seen, mountains never before climbed, the earth primordial—all of Creation, past, present, and future, was available to Donovan at a single thought, and still the world of the supernatural felt—well, agonizingly empty.

If only Aria were there, holding him, whispering in his ear—she'd help him make sense of all this senselessness. Heaven might wait beyond the blinding lights—or perhaps what he saw was the great abyss before the depths of darkest Hell—but the existence of neither kingdom felt real to Donovan without Aria.

It's not that Donovan hadn't bathed his soul in the light of first Creation—not that he hadn't traveled to Egypt and gazed at the same skies as the mightiest of the first pharaohs or taken in the fragrant light of the same ancient stars. It's not that he hadn't gazed upon an Eden newly minted under the canopy of Heaven or heard the cries of the prophets as they thundered through earliest Canaan. In fact, Donovan had ventured into Eternity and become one with what he could of it, weighing every ounce of Creation, experiencing all that was human and inhuman, witnessing the whole chain of the human family—and still he felt incomplete. Still, he felt pain, obsession—a ghostly adolescence of sorts in which he couldn't shake one consciousness completely for another, in which he couldn't distance himself from the other half of his twin soul.

Though Donovan could feel the presence of that spiritual family in the greater light, a stronger light captivated him, held him earthbound, that rarest luminescence that he knew only as Aria. To ask Donovan to enter into eternal rest without the very soul that brought him such repose was like asking a man to walk away from his head and heart and still be whole. It was impossible, even with all of Creation before him. Aria was Donovan, and he wouldn't presume to undertake so grand a task as blending with Eternity without all of her consciousness accompanying him.

No, he must descend towards that light—if only to grieve that its fire had diminished, that its brilliance had grown starkly divided. There was a new, steady vibrancy belonging to a lesser light, belonging to another man. While examining the future from every last angle and seeing the bits and pieces of the life the two would share, Donovan couldn't help but disapprove of Creation itself for allowing this. This dull man had none of the radiance of Earth's most brilliant point of light, of Aria. Instead, Aria must join with him, and he with her, for the fount of their eternal love to remain unpolluted.

But how to speak to her, with his new, greater voice—how to make the voice of Heaven heard by the ears of Earth?

Not even Donovan knew the answer to that one. And so, he simply perched by Aria's bed, simply whispered through the mirror, simply hovered near her, gathering in the seaside scent of her perfume. He simply existed by her, near her, but not in her, incessantly waiting.

Nothing Donovan ever said to Aria quite said I love you like his waiting.

Aria had had many lovers, but Donovan never quite struck up a connection to the graces of other women. To him, Aria was all that was female, and other girls were simply pale imitations of a priceless original he couldn't stop gazing at, couldn't put down. If Aria had one regret, deep and abiding, above all others, it was that she had wasted so many years on momentary bliss when she could've spent those years, those days, each of those seconds, by the side of the man who'd ultimately know so few.

To this day, as she packed him away like the last of the boxes before her, Aria was touched by the embers of memory that reignited her passion nightly. She grew fond of the reminisces of Donovan standing in the high school parking lot, always near the same beaten Dodge sedan in case Aria needed a ride home. It was such an elegant gesture, romantic in its simplicity. For Donovan knew Aria, the whole Aria, of present, past, and future. He remembered when she was simply a small first-grade child, of how she perpetually awaited her mother or some other parent, lamenting about how nice it'd be to simply have someone to take her home.

In the end, that someone was always Donovan.

Standing, waiting, as Aria made her way through high school graduation despite less than caring parents. Attentive when she needed a lift to and from college classes after she'd wrecked her own car from myriad stupid stunts on countless dates she'd long since forgotten. It was Donovan standing, awaiting her once more as she walked down the aisle to take his hand.

That, more than anything else, was how Aria pictured Donovan: her umbrella in the rain, her blanket in the night, her watcher, her protector.

And so, despite all the stories of murder, of spectral bloodletting, fueling the media, Aria still knew in her heart that all Donovan could ever do was try to see her home.

Standing, sealing those memories with the last boxes of the house that would've held their marriage, Aria felt guilty, truly guilty, that she couldn't wait through a small thing like the ages of her life for the man who'd always meant eternity to her.

CHAPTER 14:

Duet To Violin

⌒ Ironic, this packing of boxes.

Not six months ago Wallace would've thought the prospect of Aria leaving her shrine to Donovan impossible.

And with good reason, considering the long history Wallace shared with the outer reaches of Aria's abode. After finally making it inside, Wallace witnessed Aria's original wedding firsthand through the assortment of photos Aria attempted to hide in select passages throughout the house. At first, she'd blush ever so slightly, claiming she had forgotten to remove one photo or another as she showed off her budding botanical efforts. But even a man as oblivious to the intricacies of the female heart as Wallace knew that with women, there were no accidents. The photos existed near an old kitchen table, beside a medicine cabinet, or by her purse, for a reason.

The pictures became a ritual of sorts. At first, Wallace averted his glance away from the photos of bride and groom. Then, after asking politely and piecing bits of the story together, he decided to recruit the pictures, to make gifts of elaborate albums that might win Aria into opening the gates to this netherworld she lived in.

Aria grew perpetually silent, unwilling to commit sacrilege to the governing philosophy of her life, one of reverence for a dead past. Still, she allowed Wallace's insistent questions, realizing, only just now, that part of her wished to break from those pictures, to walk out and come alive in her flesh once again. It was that part of Aria that finally handed Wallace Donovan's old key, that finally made her house a home again.

"Are you sure?" Wallace asked dutifully, holding the key snugly for show. He knew how much the simple gesture meant and how obligated he, as the receiver, was to let Aria know he appreciated and understood.

"It's time," Aria said less than convincingly, the color dimming in her eyes. "Time I let this old place go."

"Old?"

She tucked the last of the pictures away, the pale, strapless dress she wore mocking her more than Donovan's arm resting so naturally over her exposed shoulder.

"To me it is. Wallace, I love you, but I hope you realize that a year without him has been like a lifetime alone. This house was my tomb."

Wallace stepped closer, cradled her with one arm.

"There's always room—"

Aria pulled away, stepping towards the forgotten light of the sun. "Just give me one last week here," she said. "I'll turn my key over to the realtor on Friday."

"Just tell me—whatever it is, whatever you feel, just—"

Aria turned to Wallace, eying his uneasily combed hair, his frantic black eyes, eying him, uncertain.

"I can't—I just can't find any words big enough to capture what I lost. Just understand. Just give me until Friday."

The husband-to-be knew his role, nodding deferentially to his long-suffering wife.

꙳ The more Wallace watched the six o'clock news, the more he became convinced that Aria might just be in danger.

In fact, it took the seeming objectivity of broadcast news to make him admit that such a thought had ever crossed his mind. Despite the strange sensations he felt in his last nights in the apartment, Wallace could not freely admit that he believed in anything remotely supernatural. Still, the bizarre cuts he sometimes received, lassoing his flesh, the loud, banshee-like cries, the endless feeling of a presence in his most private hours, all rattled him more than he'd ever care to admit to Aria.

Police suspect an arsonist may be on the loose in Burgundy Hill, a small upscale coastal community that hasn't seen a crime wave of this magnitude in thirty years, the female anchor rattled on.

Wallace watched as the anchor's bleach blonde bangs caught the light of the studio, as her black eyes, so apathetic, somehow seared the words she spoke into his memory.

A rash of house fires has swept the small community, all accompanied by a signature red fog that area scientists cannot explain.

The camera cut to a local resident, a rotund woman with large glasses and speckled hair of matted gray. *We don't know what it is; it could be a chemical of some kind,* the interviewee suggested.

Police are asking the community for any—

At that moment, Wallace heard the announcer's voice turn to static as tiny black and white dots paraded across the screen. He looked out the window to see the encroaching fog, an abysmal red and black mist that spilled deeply into the sky.

Wallace rose, searched through the darkness. "It's you," he could hear himself mouthing. "Every time I think you're an illusion, here you are."

Wallace could feel a set of eyes upon him, a leery blue, watching from some distance veiled by time and mortality.

"If you lay so much as a hand on her—"

Wallace could not complete the line. His throat writhed, turned pink, then purple. He choked, collapsing to his knees as the red fog consumed him.

She's my wife eternal, he could hear, feel something suggest.

Wallace refused to buckle to something as nonsensical as a ghost.

"I, I love her," he coughed out, as he struggled to regain balance. "You won't hurt her—not again. That I promise you."

Even as he spoke the last words, Wallace felt some force propelling him against a pale ocher wall. The thrust was so quick, so violent, he felt the ghoul simply eying him, observing the results of the crashing of skull and bone.

I don't want to hurt you, the supernatural voice said. *Just leave. Don't tempt me. I can't control what I'm becoming.*

Wallace collected his breath, stood up. He felt the supernatural pain emanating from the wounded spirit. For a moment, he could almost see the blue fire of the eyes that this shadowy fog of a presence possessed. The agony was excruciating and very real.

Even so, the burn of humiliation was upon him, and he articulated only: "I *will* marry her."

A wail, a rage of fire and noise, something like the cry of a dying child, broke out as the ghost lifted Wallace to the air in a supernatural choke, then tossed him against the wall. As the mortal lost consciousness, he could almost see the specter looming over him, debating whether to finish the job.

Having recovered enough to treat his own wounds, Wallace sat staring at the giant dent in the wall. Had he truly been propelled against it? Had a ghost, a wounded soul of some kind, avenged itself upon him? Wallace smirked at the absurdity of the premise, but that gaping dent, so definite in the natural world, wiped that smirk away quickly enough.

Wallace reminded himself that the issue here wasn't simply coming to terms with a ghostly attack; it was protecting Aria. For a brief moment, Wallace contemplated honoring the ghost's request. He considered leaving Aria, once and for all, picturing his life without the touch of her hand. At that thought, he could almost feel, in some quantifiable form, how much the spirit truly loved Aria. The whole power of the emotion emanated from him, as it had from the ghostly assailant.

Unquestionably, Wallace had a hard time picturing that the ghoul had the same treatment in store for Aria that it had for him, but there was one undeniable truth: not only was the spirit alive, but it was also violent, inescapably so. By its own admission, if Wallace had indeed sensed its message correctly, it could not control its rage. Wallace sympathized with the spirit and if he were not so jealous, might even have apologized for saying so callous a remark in response to the spirit's efforts to make him understand. But tortured though the spirit was, Wallace could not just leave Aria to its whims.

It will kill her, Wallace surmised. *It would be the only way. And Aria would follow this tormented creature willingly.*

And there was the heart of his conflict: How to help a willing victim? Wallace never pretended that Aria loved him nearly so deeply as she did her late husband, though he'd fantasized about what their relationship might've been like if she had. And to be truthful, Aria was clear enough about her feelings when he first met her and fell in love.

Wallace thought of whether anything might change this. He thought of telling her all about the ghostly attack. Then he thought of Aria. She'd suffered so much already, and the matter of the wedding and reception were even at this late juncture, not entirely decided. To add this to her worries would cause not only tears, but a potential breakdown.

Sitting there, in pain, Wallace performed his first act as husband: putting his bride's needs above his own. Sure, he'd like the comfort, the solace, of sharing, not to mention any opportunity under the sun to make Donovan look insidious. But ultimately Aria would hate him for clipping the wings of her ghostly angel and not taking his pain like Donovan would have. *How odd,* Wallace thought, *that I'm her fiancé and even I think of him as her one and only.* No, this was not how he pictured his own wedding day or his marriage. But Wallace loved Aria, in his own peculiar way, and that was all that mattered. He must be a husband first, even if that put his needs as a man last.

So what to do now? What would a responsible husband do for his wife? Wallace wondered. Granted, Wallace was tempted to call his insurance company— though he was not quite sure what he'd report—and maybe contact a repairman of some kind—whoever it is that mended walls ghosts destroy. But that would help his landlord and himself only. And so, Wallace picked up the phone and placed the first call to the rectory of the church Aria attended, waiting until he had its old monsignor, Father McDonald, on the line.

How Aria, even in her slumber, remembers that other wedding—not the day in the church, but the day of her actual marriage.

I'm through with this, Donovan had articulated, his face flushing, his arms flying as if the wind.

Aria crouched, wiped the crimson face off of Donovan with a generous heaping of the sea.

I'll kill him, Donovan screamed. Hell, I'll kill myself!

Donovan's arms sought to punish wind and rock, sought to return violence to the elements.

You can't go, Aria protested. What will I do if you go?

In that one moment, Donovan became a boy again. He collected himself, wiping away his own blood, thinking of the greater abuse the world might hold for his beloved.

Follow me, he screamed, running after a snow-laden cloud.

Aria, as always, did.

The snow fell all about them, like rice at a wedding heralded by the heavens. Donovan took Aria's hand. Though only fifteen, Donovan and Aria could sense the permanence that holding hands implied, the implicit connection. They felt it in the waves, which thundered in chorus as they stood on wanton cliffs, looking to eternity below.

I want to make you believe, Donovan struggled to articulate. That I won't leave you. That I can't.

Aria understood. How does it go? she asked, rather unceremoniously.

Do you take this man, I think, Donovan added. Do you take this man to be your lawfully wedded husband... or something like that.

Lawfully? Aria asked.

You're supposed to say I do.

I do, Aria added, in complete trust. What of the rest of it?

I say the same after something about in sickness and in health, for better or for worse, until death do you part.

Just until death? Aria asked playfully.

Forever then. There will be no till death do us part.

The waves crashed in roaring approbation.

Does that mean we're husband and wife?

We always were, Donovan corrected her.

CHAPTER 15:

Solo For Strings

꩜ Donovan burned like the stars, spending his long nights looking down from the vast glory of Heaven to the one star that outshone the celestial kingdom. After Aria brushed her teeth, loosened her hair, turned out the light, and graced the sky with one last parting gaze, Donovan would often descend, setting the sky ablaze in purples and pinks to presage his coming. Aria, taken in by the unusual silky lights, looked out the window a moment longer, smiling ever so slightly before remembering the burden of her widowhood.

Donovan lived for such moments, for the ability to once again spark the smile that set Heaven on fire. But how short-lived such glory was; how quickly the fire consumed itself and was gone. As the nights passed and even the midnight splendor of the stars waned on Aria's affections, Donovan could feel the distance of eternity settling between them. He could sense from the sporadic imagery of Aria's dreams a giant undiscovered country separating the living and the dead. It was the country to which he now owed his citizenship, a gray and misty land full of all celestial wonders but, to Donovan, devoid of one mortal's warm touch.

And so, he spent his nights singing ghostly songs in Aria's sleeping ear, reminding her of his voice before the echo that was their love was lost to eternity.

The words grew, like vestiges of the past, in Aria's mind, until the voice that spoke was so nearly hers.

Even from the earliest of days, part of Donovan's intrigue was that he'd never let Aria know where he was going, a voice would whisper.

Or *There are some kisses from which a woman never recovers. Aria was blest, and cursed, to have received such a kiss.*

Donovan went on, perpetually on, the pastiches of their past in their graceful simplicity, somehow saying *I love you* and *I'll kill you* simultaneously.

To Donovan, death and sex were the same thing, one simply a euphemism for the other. To possess Aria was to kill her and awaken her all at the same time. And so, watching Aria's dreams turn to images of him as he first carried her across the threshold, of laughs and caresses from some well-lit cove caught between Aria's world and his, the desire to possess, to kill this earthly beauty surged within him.

Deep inside her unconscious self, Aria sensed the danger and the passion and was drawn towards it as she had been to that boy along the shores of yesteryear. She saw all the images of their journeying together, until the images shattered all that was not of their life together, until Aria, even in her uneasy sleep, sought to shatter the material world.

~ The next morning Wallace arrived with the utmost punctuality, a man of business down to the last detail. He had arranged for the agent to give the house a once over before the new owners came at the first of the month. Aria had agreed that any last unboxed items in the place were to be kept in exquisite order, the tables and chairs dusted, the grandfather clock polished. Had he not given up half of his weekend, despite pressing claims, to help her achieve just that goal?

What were the odds, the numbers, the stats, that would show the likelihood that the entire house would be, for lack of a more eloquent term, trashed. Oddly, the targets of the calamity had been confined to any representation of his dearly won life with Aria.

"Aria," Wallace called from the living room den.

Aria stepped down from her room, unnaturally exhausted. Her eyes met Wallace's before he could ask about the state of the house, but barely saw him, so huge were the wells of black developing in oblong circles beneath them.

"What happened last night?" Wallace asked innocuously.

"I haven't slept in days," Aria confessed with a painful yawn.

She collapsed in the nearest available chair, a mere puddle of flesh barely animated by life.

"I don't understand what that has to do with—this," Wallace indicated with a sweep of his arm.

Wallace walked over the broken glass, towards her, just standing there, observing this anomaly in the universal order that up until now had governed their relationship.

Aria looked up, seeking confidence.

"I've seen—things," she said vaguely. "First in the night sky. Now here."

"Did you see how this mess got made?"

Aria looked down, her eyes resting upon Wallace's crooked smile as it stared back at her from broken glass.

"If you're still having second thoughts—" Wallace said in a broken cadence.

"No," Aria protested. "It's just that—sit down."

"The realtor will be here at any moment!"

"Sit down," Aria ordered.

The harshness of her tone commanded the utmost compliance from her husband-to-be.

Aria looked through her weariness at the man seated in front of her.

"I'm going to tell you something, and it's not up to you to believe me."

"What—"

"You will believe me, however ridiculous it sounds. Are we clear?"

Wallace sat on one of Aria's many boxes a good minute before nodding weakly. The flintiness of his judgmental black eyes hardly made Aria's confession easier.

"I'm not alone here."

"There's another man?" Wallace asked, anything but astonished given the mess all around him.

"There's always been another man."

A pregnant pause filled the air.

"I see."

"No, you don't. How to make you see-that's the problem."

Wallace started from his box. "If you could hurry this up so we can clean—"

"Wallace, shut up," Aria said emphatically, restraining his rising.

Wallace obliged, staring opaquely.

"The other man—he's my husband, my Donovan."

Wallace nodded. His stroked his thinning black hair, only too aware of the perpetual comparisons between himself and the deceased, comparisons that never ended in his favor.

"He's still here," Aria confided, seeking out Wallace's eyes. "I saw him last night—that is, I felt his presence. He did these things. Or at least—he did them through me."

Not so much as a hint of breath came from Wallace's composed frame. He simply reached into his breast pocket, produced a cell phone, and started dialing.

"I'm sorry to do this to you, Adam," he prattled on, turning away from Aria, "but my fiancée's in no condition to leave the house today. We can't show it. She's ill and whatever she had is all over the place."

Sharp vibrations, something like sound made tangible, emanated from the cell.

"Wallace," Aria screamed shrilly. "I'm telling you something damned important! I'm telling you my dead husband's still here and you're talking to a realtor!"

The white noise from the other end ceased.

"I'll explain later," Wallace said to the line, ending the call.

His face showed, in ruddy cheekbones, the faintest irritation at the fact that his soon-to-be bride might be insane.

"I love him," Aria confessed. "I still do. I always will. How can I tell you this? How can you understand?"

Aria sought words lost deep within herself, came up empty. Momentarily, Wallace's eyes softened as he too thought back to the first time he felt the violence of love.

"All I can say is when I first saw the sun rise, he was there. When I first learned to speak, it was his name that came from my lips. When I first started to become a woman, it was his eyes that showed me I was attractive to men. When I first learned what death was, it was through him, too. Damn it, Wallace, can't you understand? I love him, but I'm scared, damn scared."

Wallace made an effort. "Scared?" he asked, his own curiosity kindled.

"When he's angry, he's cruel," Aria continued, "terribly cruel."

Wallace smirked, a gesture not entirely inappropriate. "This is about the wedding. You're trying to get me to bump back the date, aren't you? That's what's really frightening you. Being married to me."

Aria reached for Wallace's hand, so fragile, so delicate and refined, hoping, infinitely hoping, that he might feel her hand trembling.

"This is your first test as my husband," she said openly. "It may seem impossible to you, but you have to believe me. This place is haunted. I'm haunted. I need you to help me through this. I need you to be my husband now. I need you to be strong when I get weak. I need you to have faith when I have none. And, most of all, I need you to believe and to understand."

Wallace nodded adamantly. Aria, sensing the pretense, released his lukewarm hand.

A part of Wallace wanted to confess to the horrors he'd seen, wanted to take the chance to be closer to his wife, but he felt lost in his own rationalism.

His eyes stared endlessly ahead, betraying his distance. "I'll start cleaning," Wallace said without looking at his intended.

"Damn you," Aria whispered.

As Wallace picked up the shards of glass, he saw Aria's eyes make contact with the burn adorning his hand.

"What you're telling me—it just can't happen. It makes no sense," he speculated, until his eyes caught Aria's.

Wallace turned away, but Aria's eyes assailed the man. "You've seen him too. That's it, isn't it? You've seen him and you're too cowardly to admit it, so you let me carry on!"

"Seen, maybe. Felt," Wallace said, raising his hand, "yes."

Aria approached the man, forced the glass from his hands. "What is it you felt? Tell me honestly!"

Wallace stared down the moment of his encounter, his thoughts as scattered as the shards. "It was—unnatural," he said at last.

"He threatened you, didn't he?"

"I don't want you worrying over me, especially since I don't know what I saw. I was tired. I'd been working on the sale all week," Wallace rattled off, attending to the broken glass.

Aria took hold of the smarting hand. "You're trembling," she added, pulling him closer.

"I didn't want to tell you this—I know you love him. I know he's night and day to you, but he attacked me," Wallace said, sounding for all the world like a tattling toddler. "I don't believe in these things, but somehow, it happened."

"My God."

"Can you imagine my fear now? The idea of you in this house, alone—"

"With him?"

Wallace's lips trembled in confession. "With it—"

"I don't fear him."

"I know," Wallace said, holding up his scarlet scar before Aria's translucent eyes. "That's what scares me."

Aria pecked the bristles of his cheek.

"That's why I called your priest," Wallace said.

Aria paused in her action, pulled away. "You what?!"

Wallace caught her eyes. His eyes were now like a child's seeking comfort, solace, security. "Well, I didn't reach him, exactly," he insisted. "But I left a message. I said it was urgent that I speak with him. He hasn't called back. At least, not yet."

"You should've told me first. I am your fiancée, Wallace!"

"I'm sorry—it's just I don't know what I saw, what I heard, what I felt. I just know I don't want you to see or hear or feel the same thing, whether it's a ghost or simply anxiety. I just want it to all go away."

"I understand."

The two looked at each other, commiserating in their silence.

"I know him," Aria asserted. "He is real, very real. He's not a monster, not the killer ghost the media makes him out to be. He's suffering because of me. You have to understand—no priest can cure that, Wallace. Only I can help him find peace."

"Not at the cost of—" Wallace stammered, struggling with the thought. "Let me stay."

"That will only anger him and put you at further risk," Aria said in genuine concern. "I have to do this alone."

"I can't just grab my keys and walk out," Wallace confided, sounding almost like a scolded child.

"Then allow me," Aria said, gripping his keys, then handing them to him.

Wallace stood for a moment, as still as the grandfather clock that rang in the hour.

"He'll be here soon," Aria told him, prodding him off and on with her words.

"I can't just go."

"You have to accept that you have no control in this," Aria told him. "It's not a claim you can handle or a book you can balance."

Wallace's eyes flashed in antipathy. "I didn't say—"

"Have a careful drive home. I love you."

Shaking his head, Wallace stumbled for his old consort, the door.

"I'm doing this for us," she said.

"Are you sure which us you're referring to?"

"This will be my wedding gift to you and my anniversary present to him," Aria said.

"Just be clear," Wallace said before leaving, "which one of us is the ghost and which the husband."

∽ That night, Aria fought to keep her eyes open for her ghostly caller, only to be reminded of the remote silence that had become her life in his absence. Though she couldn't explain the feeling, her whole body trembled with the subconscious urge to return to the cemetery, to feel in its cool slate the tangibility of lost love.

But Aria fought the feeling, just lying there, in her own cemetery—her purple bed—wondering how she'd manage work, a move, and a wedding while fighting a fiancé with no panache and a mother with far too much. Her eyes became silky beads of pearl polished by the thin veneer of sleep. Her body became as still as if in a moratorium. Suddenly, breaking the dullness of her near slumber, was the stark, naked feeling that she was being buried alive. Aria fought to jump up, but couldn't move, visualizing her body lowering, envisioning the first heaping of black soil upon her. Just as suddenly, she felt not aridity, but warmth, as she felt herself quite literally in a bed of roses.

Still, Aria struggled to rise, to return to the land of the living. She took in the stale quiet, the settling of darkness, all over her, convinced that all was a dream until a small spark of brilliant, burning white became a shower of light before her. She saw the light take the form of a rose, first one only, enlarging, then a sea of roses raining down in a storm of flora. The lightning took her, curling like a summoning finger, until she stepped out from her first-floor bedroom, until she circled in the falling thundershower of roses.

You can hear me, can't you? she asked in her mind.

The wind answered, blowing, in small wisps of cold air, the vaguest hints of affirmation.

You're still here. You never left, Aria insisted. *It's really you.*

She reached out. The affirming winds quieted, until a malignant silence, with the weight of incessantly staring eyes, gazed from behind the shadow of the raining roses. Aria could see two misty eyes, madly blue, too deep to be human, too powerful in their gaze to be anything else.

I want to help you, she whispered to the eyes. *I want you to be at peace.*

The eyes became pools of night, their blue spilling out to an apathetic horizon as they became part of the earth. Aria, sensing their urgency, stepped out and into the night of raining roses. She navigated her way through wisps of purple petals and thick thorns, following the deep imprint the haunted eyes left upon the night. She treaded through cascading rain, mist, and flora, through streets devoid of cars, through all the earth, it seemed, not even feeling her feet beneath her, only her fingers as they pricked themselves upon the rust-colored cemetery gate.

There the two eyes of deepest sapphire again appeared. Aria was not sure whether she forced the gate or some greater force opened it for her, only that the eyes flickered, became an intense, bloody shade of red, then were lost to the mist.

You are my wife, Aria felt herself saying. She repeated Donovan's last mortal words: *There will be no till death do us part.*

Her feet approached the last of the roses, now covered in a bloody hue that preserved them. She curled up around the grave, upon the roses, which by now made up a new wedding bed. Though she fought, her legs quivering to remain solid underneath her, like a tiny girl starved for affection, she sunk into the bed, half-conscious, contemplating the smell of a thousand springs that held her even on the cusp of winter. There she laid, warmed by the wash of memory that overtook her subconscious, tucking her in as she slumbered.

From the darkest of dreams, Aria could see Donovan walking forward, not as ghost, but as man.

Valentine's Day descended. The early a.m. hours. The wind took the shape of tiny mountains of snow laying stake to the sky. As Aria enjoyed her last minutes of rest, Donovan's sienna Jeep Cherokee cut through the white wilderness, stopping nearby a more pedestrian store whose bouquets of yellow and pink roses, completely out of season, caught his eye.

Flurries of people blew everywhere, rivaling the snow flakes for dominance of land and sky. Donovan opened the jeep door, a small, notarized paper that would've been Aria's first anniversary present clutched closely in hand. In her dreams, Aria had the troubling habit of always being able to make out even the smallest of words. She knew the paper was really a deed of sale, finalizing the purchase of the Cape-style house she so adored, but which they could hardly have afforded. Donovan had cleaned out his life savings, meager as his account was, to help round out the $25,000 down they needed in order to avoid being caught in loans for the rest of their lives. The house was to be theirs. The dream of a family might soon be as well.

But even for Donovan, the gift of a lifetime was not enough. He needed something to jazz up the slip of paper, something to express the love Aria already knew he had. And so, he had to stop for flowers. For roses, specifically long-stemmed baby breath roses, whose brazen pinkness had rivaled the roses she had used daily to decorate his grave.

Donovan had just made the purchase when he stepped out of the small shop, his eyes caught on a snowy light. Aria screamed in the dream for Donovan to cease in his plans, to get back in the jeep, and when all else failed, to take just a few steps back. Had Aria been there, had Donovan been at any other spot, he might've lived.

But as fate or some darker forces might have it, Edward Stevenson, a trucker of thirty years, was about to make his first kill in that precise location. Aria could see the ice that his truck, full of Burgundy Hill assorted fudges and flowers for the nearby retail store, was to hit, could see his eyes drooping as he made the last Valentine's-related delivery at six a.m. that very morning.

How gentle Donovan's body was, so easily broken and knocked asunder as the truck made contact. The roses flew everywhere. Like the deed, they feasted on his falling blood.

His lips were so close to forming her name, so close to calling her, when the telephone rang and the Aria of a year ago undertook the grim task of picking it up.

CHAPTER 16:

Interlude

෴ Wallace said nothing as he and Aria drove out of the cemetery gates. It's not that words weren't there. It's just that they couldn't quite formulate into an expression of coherent thought. One word might capture the essence of anger, but how could that word also capture love? Wallace wondered if Aria's increasingly bizarre behavior had anything to do with his undeniable distance. Still, he kept quiet, honoring the role Aria had come to expect of him.

Aria stared out at the sky as at the great beyond. Wallace could see contemplation wrapped in the dim pupils of her eyes. He sensed that a whole world stood between them, a world that might have but a single name.

"Aren't you even going to ask?" Aria inquired.

The words hung loosely in the air. Wallace could almost see each letter dangling over him, teetering in an accusing air.

"What is there to ask?" he replied.

"Your fiancée's sleeping by a grave and you don't even think that's a subject for conversation?"

Wallace kept to his driving, saving his consternation for the 1,045,003 possible hazards of the road.

"I saw him," Aria declared. "Just last night."

"And how does that justify throwing yourself upon a grave?"

This time it was Aria who grew silent.

Wallace attempted to catch her eyes, but, unable to do so, simply shook his head. "Your mother's taken the liberty of calling your boss," he said. "She wanted me to tell you that she added a few personal days to your number. It'll mean less honeymoon time, if—"

Aria's head whipped around. "If," she repeated, fishing for Wallace's now elusive eyes.

Wallace kept himself cool, kept his eyes staring at the hardness of the road ahead of him. "You're in no shape for a wedding," he offered. "Your mother disagrees with me, but—"

"But?"

"All my life I never asked for much," Wallace said, steadying the wheel. "But one prayer that was mine since the age of ten was to have a woman who'd love me, who'd put me first."

In one sharp stab of motion, Aria turned away. "You knew how I felt about him when we first met. I never lied."

"You didn't," Wallace admitted, "but I did. I thought yesterday—I thought when I shared what he did to me—it'd mean something to you."

"Of course it did!"

"Really?" Wallace let the word linger between them. "You said you'd come to say goodbye, but the woman I saw curled up on that grave isn't saying goodbye to the ghost. She's saying goodbye to me."

"It wasn't like that. Something just, well, possessed me."

"Did you know, Aria, that in my line of work I deal with widows and widowers all the time? Nearly 62.5% of all those that hold our life insurance policy sign a new beneficiary within five years. That beneficiary is another spouse."

"How. . .efficient they are."

"Aria," Wallace said, stopping the car. His lips wavered, as if stumbling to express something devoid of the wonderful world of statistics. "I work in life insurance because I know how sloppy life is. I accept that sloppiness. But that doesn't mean I didn't have dreams of my own. I'm thirty-five, Aria, with good savings and a good income. And with no wife and no family. I may never dash a woman away to the beach or give her a rose each day of her life. Those thoughts may not occur to me nearly as much. But that doesn't mean I have nothing to give."

"I want to marry you," Aria insisted. She reached out, gently touched Wallace's cheek.

Wallace withdrew from her touch. "Nearly 55% of all marriages of the past ten years have failed within four years," he replied.

"And how are you so certain? Was there a change in beneficiaries?" Aria quipped.

"Because that's human nature," Wallace said by way of reply. "People build castles in the sky without securing their foundations here on earth. You and Donovan did that. And it worked. You escaped that divorce. You escaped the statistics! And it's unfortunate, what happened. I grieve for you; really, I do. But his death shouldn't be yours."

"What the hell is that supposed to mean?"

Wallace pulled into Aria's driveway. How empty the cool pavement and adjacent house looked in the light of day, how naked.

"I could've given you children, a family," Wallace stammered out. "I could've been a good husband."

Aria opened the car door, but sat in disbelief. "You still can be."

"Your mother's expecting you," Wallace asserted. "I called her on the cell just after I saw you lying there, by his grave."

"Will I see you later? Will we talk?"

The pain sat so vividly on Wallace's stoic countenance, limned into his cheeks and wrinkles. "I told you last time, Aria, that whatever I've seen, whatever I've felt, I can't bring myself to believe in ghosts. Let's just say I don't plan on becoming one."

∞ Ironically, Bella's premature cheer over a wedding that might never occur was the only joy Aria came to know. All of nature was afoul. Storms and fog brooded over near and far shores, consuming the coastal community in an epidemic never before seen, and yet all Bella cared for was the wedding. She seemed to think that whatever drove Aria to that cemetery, whatever drove her to Donovan, could be cured by the simple act of walking an aisle with another man. Perhaps that's why Aria had acquiesced to her mother's whims. For all her reservations, Aria hardly wanted to lose the hall twice and double the insult to her intended. In fact, that compassion was the very card Bella held and inserted perfectly into the mix, knowing that the one gesture would likely finalize the marriage once and for all.

Still, as Bella finished reporting that the bridesmaids had all received their catalog dresses, specially ordered at Bella's own expense for the event, even she could see that Aria's focus was far off, across distant horizons.

"You haven't said a word," Bella said, still reveling in the quality of the bridesmaids' ensemble.

"You haven't let me."

"I'm asking, aren't I?"

"I think Wallace left me."

Bella dropped the catalog. Its exposed pages, lavishing one smiling bride after another, spilled openly across the floor.

"I wasn't planning on going back on Wallace again, but this wedding, Mother, it still feels like a funeral."

"It doesn't have to be, if you'd just. . ." Bella felt it on the tip of her tongue, the harangue about her daughter's questionable behavior: harolding in cemeteries and taking far too long to move. She wanted to explode, but Bella, perhaps seeing some of her own blood in her daughter after all, did not come back with a barrage of reasons for Aria to wed. She simply asked: "To hell with the yelling. I've yelled and cried enough over this. Just answer me this, Aria: Do you love Wallace? Do you want what's best for him?"

"Of course," Aria said. Tears wet the blush on her cheeks. "I'm just not sure what that is anymore."

Bella sat on a packed box next to her daughter, offering a tissue for Aria to clean up the wet residue of her makeup. Aria obliged.

"There was a time I felt the same way about a man, before I even met your father," Bella confessed.

Aria looked through her tears at her mother's surreptitious smile.

"I was engaged to him. The date was set."

Curiosity got the better of tears for a moment, as Aria asked: "Who was he?"

"A local."

"Is he still alive?"

"Very much alive."

Bella paused a moment. There was more in that pause than Aria heard in her words.

"I'd never loved so much. He was witty, tall, with a wiry build and these blue eyes that opened up to the sky."

"Mother."

"I'd have married him in a heartbeat. Maybe if I had there wouldn't have been all those divorces."

Aria searched out her mother's opaque eyes. This time it was Bella who fought back the tears as Aria asked: "What happened?"

"He had to choose," Bella said, her caesura of sorts accentuating her pain, "between God and me."

"And God won?"

"Doesn't He always?"

Aria smirked.

"I loved him as much as I loved your father, Aria, if not more. But I let him go. I let him go because I loved him. I knew he'd never forgive me if I didn't make the choice for him. And so I did. That's what women are, Aria: stronger than men. We're the strength of the world, really, and don't let anyone tell you otherwise. I can tell you from too much experience that you have to be strong, Aria, because you'll never find that strength in men."

"So what are you saying? That I should let Wallace go?"

"Only you can say that for sure. What I'm saying is that love is many things, Aria, and none of them easy. A bride must put her groom first, which may be why I've been in so many divorces. In the end you have to ask: What's better for Wallace, dear? If you ask me, I'd say that's a life with you."

Bella got off the box, reached over for her purse.

"I don't know, Mother. I just don't know," Aria said, drying her eyes.

"Love's not about having the answer. It's about being open to the questions. Ask yourself. Your heart will let you know."

Aria reached out for her mother's hand. Bella took her daughter's.

"Let me know if I need to call the bridesmaids and tell them to save their time and efforts."

"I will," Aria promised.

"And talk this over with Wallace once he cools off. There's nothing colder than making a groom a stranger to his bride."

The night of Donovan's passing had been a storm unto itself, very much the equal to the thunder and lightning that presently held Aria's body and mind captive.

In the echoes of wind, and the torrents of rain and hail, Aria could still hear the raspiness of Donovan's voice the very moment she finally made it to the hospital where he'd been taken to die.

How cruel she felt it was of her beloved's soul to use this vision, this reminder of the pain she'd only recently begun to heal from. But Aria could not turn away.

The doctors had moments before they stopped concerning themselves over Donovan, reasoning that they'd contained his bodily fluids as best they could given the force of the impact.

Weakly, he'd gazed up at his young bride, an absence in his eyes. It was as if he'd still been searching for the roses he'd planned to bring her hours earlier, each representing a month of the marriage that had only this day grown a year old.

"What an anniversary present," he'd said more than asked, the smile teetering on his lips punctuating his point.

"Just lie still," was all Aria could manage to muster.

"It's just not fair, not a damn bit of it," Donovan argued, as Death stood before the young man's fading vision. "I won't stand for any of it. I said I'd be a husband for life. I said I'd give you a baby."

At that moment the thunder weighed in, adding to the spectacle Donovan made in the hospital room.

"I won't just let go," he argued to no one in particular.

"But you're in too much pain." Aria sobbed openly. She collected her next words carefully. "If you have to go, go, my love. I'd live a thousand lives of pain for you to feel one moment of peace."

"I won't die. I won't leave you," Donovan decided, reaching up limply with his chilling hand. "Take my hand."

Aria obliged, kissing the united fist that had always been theirs, their last defense against a remorseless world.

"I will live on as our love," Aria's dying husband prophesied. "I will not let our love die. There will be no till death do us part—"

And that was it.

Just as Donovan had fought his way into this world—had fought his way through it—he fought his way out of it. Always getting the final world, in an argument they'd never have the chance to resolve.

Had the stubborn man lived but moments longer, maybe he would have seen the acceptance, the love, that Aria so desperately sought to translate into touch, to make him feel, to make him understand.

He didn't need to worry about preserving their love. Aria was its temple, and in her, no matter what else happened, it would survive.

Listening to this storm for the ages, caught between two worlds, Aria felt not so much the rage and anger as the desire to take the crying childlike ghost she sensed around her, to hold him until all the fury of thunder and lightning passed, until this boy-man she had so adamantly loved was at rest in the arms of eternity.

Part 2

CHAPTER 17:

Cadenza

∽ As Donovan watched from outside the window, he saw stars drift away, disappearing through the drapery of the nighttime clouds. He imagined he knew how they felt, that he might soon be lost among them.

How frequently Donovan reached out to Aria. How often he braided her hair back from the edge of the bed so that it might not be caught between pillow and post. How he made certain the bathroom door was open so that, when rushing to work in the morning, Aria might not stumble into it as she had during their brief year of marriage. How much of an effort he put into making sure she had her scarf in a visible place so that she wouldn't forget it and grow cold, as she always found a way to do.

The tragedy of Donovan's life was as simple and unmovable as the distance he felt in Aria. How much he whispered words of love in her ear. How frequently he, even in death, honed his feelings, searching out just the right vibrancy of authentic emotion to resonate with his beloved. How he longed to let her know that he was still present, that he still cared, that he had come—for her.

But each morning Aria awoke, sweeping her hair from the pillow, rushing to the bathroom, wrapping the scarf around her before she left, Donovan could feel her a world removed. However much he fought to say the smallest, meaningful piece of verbiage, to offer up, in intense introspection, the most profoundly acute feeling of love he might muster, Aria was perpetually walking away. In the early months, it got to be that he recognized her only from behind, when her feet carried her to some other world, farther and farther, until all that remained was an empty house and its empty portraits. The indignity of being forgotten incensed the ghoul. As Donovan watched Aria walking, he knew that the time was near—that he must strike.

 ☙ *Did I ever truly know him?* Aria thought to herself the next day as she sat catching morning light on the edges of *The Burgundy Herald*. Awaiting Bella's arrival, she read the press captions calling the apparitions of Burgundy Hill the worst recorded case of a haunting in local history. Monstrous orbs of light, semi-human faces, generic tricks of light, all garnished the tabloid pages as eager reporters speculated on the identities behind the nightmarish ghouls lording over the cemetery. Surely enough, because of the date of his death, her Donovan was included in the number.

Aria tried to finish her bacon omelet, to pull herself together enough to review the napkin arrangements Bella had left with her. How quickly the most definitive moment of her life, from the church hosting the ceremony, to the hall hosting the reception, had been decided. All Bella had trusted the sickened Aria with was napkin arrangements, which even now were being decided upon all too late. Aria was supposed to have an answer, supposed to accompany Bella to rehearse the steps of her wedding march with the local pastor, Father McDonald, to prepare for the day now less than a full week away. And yet, all she could find herself thinking of was whether Donovan had ever been more than illusion all along.

I do remember him, Aria thought. Not so much the beauty as the barbarity of the boy she loved took hold of her thoughts. Screaming, threatening, smashing glasses, hurtling rocks—all these had accompanied the wounded boy wherever she saw him. In one case, after she came home from college from yet another tryst, Donovan had awaited her, stalking the shadows that accompanied her steps. He'd grabbed hold of her arm, tightly, cursed at her with a litany of vulgarity she'd never heard before. Aria understood that he was wounded, that it was she who wounded him. Yet, the words shed light on a side of the man she had discarded so long ago. He could be angry, so angry. *He could get angry enough to kill,* Aria thought, *if he didn't get his way.*

Still, thoughts of Donovan cradling the wounded horseshoe crab, carrying her from the shores when she was wounded, staying with her after her father missed the birthday, making a cake in the beach sand—all of these spoke of such a gentle soul. How could the ghoul that took its own abusive father's mortal life and the boy who jokingly blew out sand candles for Aria be the same person? *Did I ever truly know him? Did I ever know him at all?* The question lingered the moment Bella, without knocking, marched through the door, selecting the napkins for Aria as Aria arose, preparing for the march that would lead her to the rest of her life.

꩜ In decades past, Father McDonald had waged a battle against an absolute evil most had long since dismissed as medieval myth. He had seen the powers of demons, felt their attacks waking him from his sleep at night. He didn't always see them in their hideous forms, but he smelt the foul sulfur of their ancient, hellish incarnations and knew the hissing breaths that taunted him. In a peculiar way, he almost considered such attacks a badge of honor, as they meant to him that the powers of Hell considered him a formidable adversary they wished to expel by any means necessary.

Though Father McDonald had heard the possessed utter languages new to the earth, though he had seen the excruciating marks and bloody lashes on the bodies of the victims, he had never quite seen or heard of anything like whatever it was that possessed Burgundy Hill. Whatever power controlled ghosts that he'd never believed in or seen, unleashing them upon a helpless town, was by far more powerful than anything he'd commanded to the depths of Hell. And to hear the earnestness of the young man on the phone who truly believed he'd been attacked by the master force behind all the murders, diabolical fogs, and specters terrorizing the community was truly astonishing. For weeks, Father McDonald had been praying his rosary, attending reconciliation, and fasting as he collected missives from his bishop urging caution and neutrality until Rome weighed in on the situation. Now, with this Wallace Stevens, Father McDonald had the link he needed that might urge his bishop to authorize the rites of exorcism. Now, at last, Father McDonald would not be quietly preaching from the pulpit. Now, he would be the word of God in action.

Still, as he sat, reviewing his notes from the call, Father McDonald had to confess that the story didn't entirely add up to one of demonic possession. First and foremost, there was no demon to be found, merely the angered spirit of a man who apparently couldn't let go of his earthly bride. The power Wallace attributed to this apparition was no short of magnanimous: appearing in fire, disappearing at will, lethal strength, moving objects of any size, shrieking like a banshee, creating storms and mists, even reading minds and entering into the thoughts of others. All of these sounded like the traits of a dignitary from Hell, yet Father McDonald vaguely remembered the man they were attributed to, a man who was anything but a demon brought to earth.

Donovan Lee was a poor boy, the son of a drunk, who was more withdrawn than reckless. To the old priest, he was the poster child for broken and abusive families. A nice if somber child at first, Donovan had a mystical power in his eyes that even then conveyed his doom. He was one of those who simply weren't meant for the world, who were too proud, too sensitive, too spiritual for their own good. Father McDonald strived, but ultimately failed, to remove the child from his abusive home, and so Donovan had grown sullen and jaded from his early teenage years on.

After that, Father McDonald saw little of the child, until he administered the sacrament of marriage, and by then the boy had changed so much that the priest wondered if his soul were already gone. In Aria, it seemed, he found his salvation, and it was a shaky salvation at best.

No, this troubled boy-man could not be the force of such ancient evil unleashed upon the world. If he was involved at all, he was a pawn of greater powers that threatened the world anew. Father McDonald sat back a great while, sifting through his memories of exorcisms of the past. There, the evil had been absolute and pronounced, easily decipherable to priest and man alike.

Was it possible for Man to show some of the same evils, even after he'd passed? Father McDonald was understandably curious. He picked up the phone and dialed this Wallace Stevens, all the while importuning God to let wisdom shine through his words.

꩜ When Wallace picked up the phone, he half-expected to hear the elderly voice of a church secretary telling him that Father McDonald could not possibly be disturbed over such a speculative issue at a time of great strife in the community. Instead, he heard Aria's broken voice, so fragile, so vulnerable, it nearly struck him as the cry of a little girl.

"I know I've been unfair to you," Aria said, as plainly as she could.

"I under—"

"Just listen," Aria demanded. "It's taken me half a night to think of what to say, and I want to say it before it's all said and done."

"All said and done?"

"Just. . .listen." Aria let the breath flow in and out of her. "You deserve more than I can ever give you."

"I never asked for more than you could give."

"But you did when you asked me to be your wife. I love him, Wallace, and I love you too."

"You love me too?"

"Don't ask for more. That's all I can give."

"Give has nothing to do with it. You're making the choice, Aria, not me."

Wallace let the drama of the moment overtake him, so much so that he muted the call coming in from the other line.

"You don't understand." Aria paused, searching for words. "He's reaching out to me. I told you that I could get through to him, that I could give him peace, as a wedding present to you, as an anniversary present to him. Well, I was wrong. The kind of peace he wants can bring you nothing but pain. I can bring you nothing but pain."

Wallace winced, but held the phone tightly. "How easily you equate him with you."

Aria paused. She then argued: "I know you think I'm choosing this, but my heart chose this Wallace, long before either of us was born. I experienced everything in this world through him. When I first saw color, it was in his eyes. When I first reached out, his was the hand that held mine. He knows that. That's why he's coming. He's getting more powerful, and he won't stop until I'm on the other side with him."

Aria fell short of breath yet again. Wallace could sense that this time it was because she was earnestly stricken.

"In life, I could temper him. I could calm him down and comfort him. In death, he's more powerful than me, and it's he that riles me, instead of me subduing him. I love you, Wallace. I can't expose you to that."

"That's not your choice to make."

"I will not choose for you to die! Don't you get it? Can't you understand? Choosing me is choosing death! He'll come for you, Wallace."

"He already has."

Aria paused. In that pause was something that might almost be called admiration for the certainty that defined Wallace's voice.

"Toying with you, no doubt," Aria ultimately said. "That's his way. But this time, he'll come for the kill. His better nature will stop him, briefly, but the beast in him will get the better of him. Just as it did when he was alive."

"I won't leave you, not to this, wedding or no wedding, wife or no wife," Wallace vowed, surprising even himself with the resolve in his words.

"I love him, Wallace. I can't hurt him. Even if it means my death." Aria openly sobbed on the other end of the line, unashamed at being overwhelmed by her tears. "Yet part of me is begging you, begging you to help me, to not give up, to stand with me against whatever comes."

"Aria!"

"This may be the last time we speak to each other for some time, Wallace. If you want to call it off, I don't blame you. Either way, I can feel him taking me over. I can feel him alive in me, eating away."

"Let me help you!"

Aria collected herself long enough to insist, "It's too late, Wallace. It was too late the day I was born. Help yourself and remember, no matter what happens, no matter what he does, I love you, Wallace, and nothing can change that, not even death."

Wallace felt the cold static of the line after Aria's last words. A sense of urgency overtook him.

He dialed Father McDonald's line again, far more emphatically, only to find the second caller was still there, that Father McDonald was trying to reach him.

For days, as great storms of fire and lightning spread out from the fog, all across Burgundy Hill, the creature that was Donovan stared, in the form of a child of the storms, at the window, reaching through eternity for Aria. Always, Aria gazed intently on the face of her window watcher, recognizing this image as one of her past. How beautiful and ugly the magnificent creature looked, a consummate portrait of the storm.

This is me, Aria could feel the ghost intimate as he thrashed through the trees and the skies, becoming the great reams of lightning. At the rise of his shadowy arms, the earth shook in its monstrosity, the waves of ocean ate at an inclement shore, the rocks of the bluffs collapsed, came rolling down, and thunder rankled the land, eaten as it was by endless rain.

This is me; this is what I am, Aria could feel the night creature cry out in thunder. She could almost hear the voiceless ghost ask for her sympathy, for her acceptance, between great throbs in the wind. There he was, as always, on the outside, gazing in.

Invite me, Aria said with her lips, feeling her lost love speaking through her. *Open yourself to me.* Aria hardly knew whether to be touched or appalled by the words before her sympathies animated her arms, and she lifted the great dividing window. Outside, the spirit of the storms appeared drenched in elements so destructive they proved beyond even his control. Aria reached out, touched his hands that quaked in thunder, speaking words of understanding, of absolution.

In the crashes of thunder, Aria could hear Donovan's voice. He was in the blackness that still stood sovereign, in the dying of starlight, in the fury of a natural world made unnatural by his loss.

And even across the Heavens Aria could see what he saw, what he became: the image of a small, pale boy, with dangling chestnut bangs gathering the smallest of shells by the largest of oceans. In the shadow of the sea, Aria could see an older Donovan standing by the child, helping him as he scoured Creation for its smallest treasures. For a moment, Donovan's eyes lifted, became the flashes of lightning.

Here was an elegy for a life that never was. Here was a testament to the son that would never be born.

Aria tossed her head, shaking it to free it of the supernatural. Still, the visions would not let her rest. She rose, looked out into the eye of the storm, sympathy, indignation brewing in the electricity of the night air.

It wasn't as if the loss of the children they might've shared didn't haunt her every moment. It's just that, unlike her preternatural lover, she knew that there was a limit to tearing the foundations of Creation.

Still, Aria held the gaze of the storm, wanting Donovan to see that, just as she had when a small girl, she shared his rage against the injustice of the world, that she would strike back.

～ The inevitable meeting of the two men was a solemn affair, each eying the other with a bizarre mix of mistrust and desperation.

"I've never seen you at Mass, and I've seen Aria far less," Father McDonald said after formal introductions.

"We're not exactly great believers," Wallace responded bluntly.

It was the type of response Father McDonald had heard hundreds of times over from former parishioners of all walks of life, one that intimated that the Catholic Church was somehow hopelessly medieval, of another age and out of touch with modern life. Father McDonald almost chuckled to himself that it was always these secular free thinkers, these advanced spiritualists and rationalists, that were the first to ask if demonic possession was indeed real and possible.

"And are you believers now?" Father McDonald asked.

Wallace nodded weakly. "If it'll save Aria's life, I am."

"Could her own husband put her in such danger?"

"It's not her husband," Wallace said tersely. "It's not even human, whatever it is. I don't know if it's possessing her yet or just the house, but whatever it is, it is evil and it's there."

Wallace could see the endless doubt, the ardent speculation, trapped in Father McDonald's shale-blue eyes.

"Listen, I know you've probably seen hundreds of people who claim something like this—"

"Thousands, actually."

"—Thousands, then."

"And only three have ever turned out to be. . . substantial claims."

"Then this is one of those three."

Father McDonald smirked. "I've heard that one thousands of times, too."

Wallace turned the blackness of his eyes to the man, made his spiel. "Father, I'm begging you," he said. "We're supposed to be married Saturday morning, as you know, and we had our whole lives planned together." Wallace let his eyes do his talking for him, trying to communicate in a gesture how much of life Aria meant to him. "She's a wonderful woman, Father, really. I just want her to put all this behind her and heal. I just want her to have her wedding day."

Father McDonald gripped Wallace's shoulder. The shoulder felt nearly as rigid and stiff as the man it helped to define. "I sympathize with you, son," Father McDonald said by way of answer. "I'll do my best to help Aria, whatever it is that's afflicting her, but I hope you realize that The Church doesn't have exorcisms on demand. It's not a fast food service. It does take time, considerable time, and verification."

"Even as Aria lies there, hurting?" Wallace shook his speckled hair, drilled his eyes into the priest's. "Then that's not much of a church you've got there, Father."

"Easy now, son. We'd be hurting her more by rushing into the matter," Father McDonald replied. He stood closer to Wallace, underscoring the significance of his words with his proximity. "If it's a physical or psychological condition, if there's any other remedy, wouldn't it be best to seek that first?"

Now Wallace was the one smirking. "We've done that," he argued, producing the requisite paperwork. "The psychologist's still typing up the final report, but other than a reactive depression. . ."

"Even that could complicate matters, slow them down," Father McDonald responded honestly.

Wallace stood holding the papers, unable to move.

"I know you're looking to me for help, immediate help," Father McDonald said, ultimately taking the ashen papers. "I'll tell you what I can do. I can visit her house. I can perform a special blessing, casting out any evil spirits. That won't require the paperwork and documentation an exorcism of the possessed will, and it'll allow me to see Aria for myself."

"When, Father?"

"As soon as you can drive me over."

⤮ Aria followed the trail of roses from her bed, past the threshold of the door, down the spiral stairs, so deliciously warm to the eye while chilling to the feet, hoping her awakening senses weren't deceiving her. She had made the same journey the night Donovan and herself first moved into the small, beaten-down Cape Cod style cottage, had beheld the portrait of a man standing there, a bouquet of roses in his hand, one for each of the sixty years he'd envisioned them spending in their castle. The only missing element was touch, the warmth only one human hand upon another can communicate.

Now, there he stood, reaching, unable to feel, undead, a swirl of light and roses, an endless stream of colors pouring forth from a robe of purest supernatural light. How glorious he looked, how forlorn, how awkward. Though spectral, something like a face, with all his distinguishing features, from the aridity of his sharp cheekbone to the sea-like glow of his boyish eyes, spoke of trial, of some exquisite pain that spilled in ruby waves all about his animated form. Even in that pain, Aria recognized the ghostly contortions of his face. She had first seen them so many years ago when he was trying to get over the awkwardness of expressing his fascination for this strange new creature he had discovered, for this remarkable invention, this mythical being called woman. Aria felt, from the ebbing rays of passionate light, that Donovan, whose eyes glanced periodically from his form to hers, was that boy once more, hovering uncertainly, fearing rejection, wondering if she'd accept him, accept this profound transformation over which he had no control. He reached out, like the first man reaching for the first woman.

Aria reached forward to touch the lost life that might have been, to reassure him, only to see Donovan reach, in all his awkwardness, right through her. In times like this she might've cradled him, allayed his fears, hushed him to sleep, this strange creature she loved, both boy and man. Now she was powerless to make the pain go away, trapped by a corporeal isolation over which she too had no control. Only her eyes could caress him, offering sympathy without understanding, expressing closeness, yet separation, the painful paradox of love.

"Can you speak to me?" she whispered, perhaps worried that the strength of voice might somehow injure his fragile new form.

Aria could see lips moving, but understood nothing. She sensed Donovan was expending an extraordinary amount of energy simply appearing before her eyes.

The moment his ghostly hand reached out, towards her, Aria implicitly understood. This ghost, her Donovan, lived on in the form of his love, keenly aware of the life he'd never have. Each stray thought from her head, each walk she'd take, each morning ritual she'd partake in, would be without him. She could see, in the overbearing light of his blue eyes, an unvarnished agony.

"Show me how to help you," Aria whispered.

In a sudden explosion of light, she saw herself slumbering in a bed of endless roses, mourned over by a somnolent moon. In the distance, she could make out the pale shadows of her mother and fiancé, and beyond them, the luminosity of Donovan. She could see that her march to the coffin was no more than a march down the aisle, a plunge into true, eternal marriage. With bursting rays of red and gold, Donovan's ethereal being was urging her, commanding her, seeking to possess all of her, from the moment she was in a cradle, to the moment she'd walk eternal. Aria felt the air rush from the room, the avalanching chokes of a raspy throat, the constriction and loss of breath, all in one sudden moment of awareness. She could feel Donovan's oppressive presence suffocating her from within. Aria knelt, but fought to gain breath, to break the bond that'd suck out her very soul.

Donovan's half-formed face, struck by her intent, became ripples of angst. Aria looked up, catching the figments of air, looking at her ghostly lover with incredible sorrow and undeniable fear. At that, the figure reached out, became a pulse of red light, then exploded into the windows, ceilings, and walls, into Aria, even, in one seismic wave of supernatural activity.

He's in pain, Aria found herself thinking as she heard an obtrusive knock upon the door. *Even now, all I cause him is pain.*

 "Aria," her fiancé called from the other side of the doorway. "Are you all right? What was that noise?"

"It's late," Aria complained, unlocking the golden latch. "You should go home."

"Not until I see that you're safe."

"You can hear my voice. I'm fine," Aria said in affirmation.

Though Aria tried to dismiss the thought, she couldn't help but imagine that she'd come so close to communicating with Donovan's spirit, so close to understanding how to alleviate his torture and his pain, only to have this un-called-for savior plodding up the walkway and knocking as if he'd bust down the door itself.

"Open up, please," Wallace pleaded.

"I just want to go to bed."

"Just let me see you."

Wearily, Aria undid the latch and opened the door.

"Do you see me?" she asked.

Aria's eyes, underlined in the blackness of conscious repose, served to make her point for her. Her thin, pale arms nearly slammed the door, but before she could fully engage them, she saw the priest of her occasional parish march right in.

Aria's eyes remained on Wallace.

"I did this for you," he insisted. "After our last conversation, I grew worried."

"I have wedding details to work out in the morning," Aria complained, skulking behind the priest.

Another deathly glare directed itself towards Wallace.

"I'm sorry, Father," Aria said, barely concealing her embarrassment and rage. "My fiancé has a way of overreacting. I really don't want to take up more of your time before Saturday."

Father McDonald held up a dignified hand, his eyes lost among the shadows and the walls of Aria's abode. "Nonsense," he said after some delay. "I'm simply here to offer a blessing upon the place, to make sure that whatever's infecting the town isn't affecting you."

Aria felt like accusing the monsignor of lying, but the child of her past wouldn't allow it.

"Please proceed, then, Father," she said, her eyes still seeking to torture Wallace with their ardent stare.

As the priest took front and center in the living room, he could smell a strange fragrance, both fair, like dandelions in spring, and sulfuric, like unrelenting fire, in one. For lack of a better terminology, he could've sworn it was a mix of blooming roses mixed with ash and flame. Father McDonald could feel a presence, faded, hidden, watching him from the source of that fire, and so he stepped forward and commenced his prayers.

"O God of goodness and mercy, to Thy fatherly guidance we commend this family, this household and all their belongings. We commit all to Thy love and keeping; do Thou fill this house with Thy blessings even as Thou didst fill the holy House of Nazareth with Thy presence," Father McDonald began, gauging the presence.

The prayer was a simple one even a lay person might recite, but it did have its power upon the elemental earth of Nepal. And yet, remarkably, not an ounce of the spirit stirred. Father McDonald could feel its unsettled presence, but a truly evil force would've countered, would've said or done some act of violence. All this force did was stand there and watch.

"Keep far from them," Father McDonald continued, "above all else, the blemish of sin, and do Thou alone reign in our midst by Thy law, by Thy most holy love and by the exercise of every Christian virtue. Let each one of us obey Thee, love Thee and set himself to follow in his own life Thine example, that of Mary, Thy Mother and our Mother most loving, and that of Thy blameless guardian, Saint Joseph."

Father McDonald paused, gathered his breath as he resumed his recitation: "Protect us and this house from all evils and misfortunes, but grant that we may be ever resigned to Thy divine will even in the sorrows which it shall please Thee to send us. Finally, give unto all of us the grace to live in perfect harmony and in the fullness of love toward our neighbor. Grant that every one of us may deserve by a holy life the comfort of Thy holy Sacraments at the hour of death. O Jesus, bless us and protect us."

Not a sign stirred. Father McDonald, circled, feeling the full magnitude of the presence, yet carried on: "O Mary, Mother of grace and of mercy, defend us against the wicked spirit, reconcile us with Thy Son, commit us to His keeping, that so we may be made worthy of His promises. Saint Joseph, foster-father of our Savior, guardian of His holy Mother, head of the Holy Family, intercede for us, bless us and defend this home at all times. Saint Michael, defend us against all the evil cunning of Hell."

Only at this did Father McDonald feel a stirring within the walls, a voice so nearly human, yet so animalistic, so primal.

"What was that?" Wallace asked, subject to the same wails.

"The blessing wasn't enough," Father McDonald said.

He turned, looked in Aria's specious eyes. "The house isn't clean."

Aria's pink lips curled. Her teeth exposed themselves. "Just leave us alone," she insisted. "Just go."

"It's him," Wallace announced, nearly tripping over his retreating feet. "That's not her speaking."

"Yet, it's not demonic," Father McDonald reasoned aloud. "It's unlike any presence I've ever seen before—not man, not ghost, not good, not evil. It's something else entirely."

At that pronouncement, a violent pale fire erupted behind Aria, illuminating her features as they became ghostly.

"I do not wish to hurt you, but I will," this frail creature warned. "Go, now. Leave me to my wife."

"What Heaven hath joined, let no man put asunder," Father McDonald called out, remembering the first time he said those words to the living Donovan. "But what Hell hath joined—"

Before he could finish the words, Father McDonald felt himself traveling through static air. His body was thrust towards the wall, nearly crucified to it, until the force released him, and he fell. The elderly priest tumbled all around, his black robes swirling in a mass of activity, until he fell through the ghostly white fire and, partially burned, hit the floor.

Standing above him was Aria, who turned to Wallace, a malicious light taking the black of her pupils. "She's my wife; she lives and dies with me," Aria's lips motioned, until a purplish glow overtook her and she too fell motionless to the floor.

CHAPTER 18:

Intermezzo

～○ Once Father McDonald recovered from his fall, everything proceeded with an unnatural ease. The violent ghoul, apparently immortalized in its love and its rage, didn't so much as flicker a light, let alone toss a representative of the celestial sovereign across the room.

The rose and sulfur stench that had both beatified and poisoned the air waned. Even Aria was permitted to walk wherever she pleased.

In his past encounters with supernatural entities, Father McDonald had seen quite a bit of caginess on the part of demons. Now, he couldn't help but feel he was seeing a spirit that was—for lack of a better term—playing dead. As a man of faith, he wanted to believe absolutely that the words coming out of his mouth were the cause of the peace, of the departure of this unruly husband to God's hands, but everything just felt a little too picturesque, a little too neat in the tying up of loose ends.

And so, Father McDonald prayed, more in exhortation to God than in exorcism: "In the Name of the Father and of the Son and of the Holy Spirit, Amen. Let God arise and let His enemies be scattered: and let them that hate Him flee from before His Face! As smoke vanisheth, so let them vanish away: as wax melteth before the fire, so let the wicked perish at the Presence of God."

Father McDonald paused; not even the air stirred as he commenced: "Judge Thou, O' Lord, them that wrong me: overthrow them that fight against me. Let them be confounded and ashamed that seek after my soul. Let them be turned back and be confounded that devise evil against me. Let them become as dust before the wind: and let the Angel of the Lord straighten them. Let their way become dark and slippery: and let the Angel of the Lord pursue them."

The prayer continued, as did the silence. Father McDonald included Wallace in the proceedings, then concluded: "From the snares of the devil, deliver us, O Lord. That Thy Church may serve Thee in peace and liberty, we beseech Thee in peace and liberty, we beseech Thee to hear us. That Thou may crush down all enemies of Thy Church, we beseech Thee to hear us."

After sprinkling holy water all about the home, Father McDonald set eyes on Aria.

"That was a highly powerful prayer I just said," he indicated to her, "invoking the great archangel Michael. Even today some still use it for exorcism. And I can see why. I've heard demons wail even at the opening words," he went on. "But today," he said, pausing to contemplate the reality of his words, "I heard nothing. Not so much as a stirring."

"Then perhaps your prayers have worked," Aria said, keeping her eyes on his.

There was something hard, elusive in her stare. Father McDonald continued to analyze her pale flesh, her thin, wiry frame for any sign of possession. Aria, sensing this, smirked, but showed no outwardly abnormal behavior.

"I'd like to follow up on this," the holy man said.

Aria kept an even keel. "As you can see, Father, I'm quite fine. I'm afraid my fiancé has exaggerated the case."

Father McDonald noticed the way Aria said fiancé. It was almost as if the mere implication that Wallace could assume such a position of honor was preposterous. There was something odd, almost too serene, about Aria. Still, Father McDonald nodded his goodbyes as Wallace walked him away from Aria, towards the door.

"Are you sure you won't let us fix you dinner after all you've done?" he persisted in asking. "It's the least we can do."

Father McDonald grabbed hold of Wallace's wrist before taking back his hat and coat.

"Keep vigilant," he told him. Wallace's wrists took on a morose red as Father McDonald added: "I've seen many demons put on the faces of angels."

Wallace smirked. Father McDonald sensed it was at the supposed quaintness of a medieval religion. He kept his grip firm.

"Even now she's—it's—watching us, through her. But you needn't worry," Father McDonald said, finally releasing Wallace from his touch. "I haven't forgotten my trip through the wall. I plan to pursue this with my bishop, to get formal permission."

"Is that really necessary, Father? We have a rehearsal in two days. We're getting married."

"I'll get approval by then. As for your rehearsal, keep it scheduled. We'll see if she willingly walks into my church. If she does, I'll be waiting. Just get her there. I'll see to the rest."

"Father—"

"Be careful. It's got her, and the wife you knew may already be dead."

Wallace thanked Father McDonald hurriedly, but couldn't help but stare after the conundrum of a man as he walked away.

∽ Father McDonald was by no means surprised by the bishop's letter, by the indication that even Rome had heard of the quaint little town and its hauntings that, through the dubious miracle of the Internet, had become front-page news on tabloid sites throughout the world. The elderly monsignor could hardly so much as check his email without some ghost hunter offering his services or some local reporter seeking to make it big with a request for any insider information the Burgundy priest might have.

But this letter bore the official Vatican seal, indeed, had been delivered from the bishop's personal secretary.

The International Association of Exorcists has a personal interest in investigating this as a matter of crisis in the one true faith, the letter read, *and seeks a full counsel with his Excellency regarding the matter. Please report on these circumstances directly so that the bishop might personally appraise the situation and report back to association before The Holy Father sends a leading exorcist in the field.*

Father McDonald smirked at this twist in fortune that brought him unexpected celebrity at too old an age. As a young priest, he hoped to be known as a progressive, a missionary of the Gospel who saw faith on all continents and would take an active role in reigniting it in parishioners the world over. As the decades fell into each other, lopsidedly, he became more convinced that such was not God's will for him, that his would be the office of monsignor, tackling parish funds, city ordinances regarding parking and waste disposal, and other practical concerns that seemed anything but sublime. Now, for his town to be known as some city of sprites, as a ghost town, a haven of demons, appalled him. It wasn't God the world was coming to see so much as the devil. Goodness lacked color, panache. It was evil that sold newspapers and now the entire legacy of the town as well.

The good father shook his head, drafting a curt reply notifying the bishop, an old seminary friend, of the dangers of coming and noting a wedding he had to attend to this coming weekend. He went on to state that indeed his parishioners, suddenly increasing in number, had reported numerous strange manifestations from the supernatural world. He kept the words purposely vague, neglecting to note that he himself had smelt the stench of the red fog that seemed to stretch endlessly from the fresh graves. He himself had felt harassed by strange voices in the night, mockingly calling his name, before the encounter that saw him tossed against the wall. Supernatural activity was off the charts and not one parishioner seemed entirely unconvinced that the dead were not rising and walking among them.

An avid reader, Father McDonald had feasted upon the pages of "The Fall of the House of Usher" and felt that perhaps even thieving a line or two from Edgar Allan Poe would better narrate the town's latest happenings, since his fiction had so clearly become fact. Parishioners noted that they could only walk so far in the cemetery before the fog became more like a wall, hovering around some grave by the sea like the speaker in Annabel Lee. Strange languages fermented the air. Eyes appeared and disappeared. The winds took to torturing the skins of the town's occupants, hurtling strange harsh hail unseasonably upon all. As if out of some Shakespearian tragedy, the world was reversing itself, begging for the restoration of divine law.

And what could Father McDonald put that might summarize the peculiar deviations from the law of the Lord? What could encapsulate the full barrage of the eerie and unnatural? Father McDonald cupped his chin with his fingers, then wrote, simply, based upon his experience in the far corners of the world,

Dear James:

Please notify Rome to send—immediately—any leading exorcist from the association that she might spare.

Truly,
Msgr. James McDonald, Reverend

ᔋ As Wallace stood upon the entrance of what was to be his and his wife's future Cape-style home, he could swear he felt the presence all about him.

He had sensed the same presence, magnified, in Aria. As he moved over the final boxes, even her eyes had a slight look of the maniacal about them, only slightly warmed over by the saving grace of life. But the presence, the stench of burning roses, became more powerful as Wallace opened the door.

Still, Wallace couldn't help but stand, looking over the cream-colored tiles, the white marble-topped counters, the large, welcoming space of the den, wet-eyed. He could hardly have admitted to himself that he was on the verge of tears, that all that he had invested his life savings in, the marriage and domicile that were to be something of a life, felt in jeopardy. How he wanted Aria to share in the moment of glory, to stand proudly gazing upon the magnificent home that, despite fluctuations in the housing market, they'd been able to successfully mortgage.

Instead, Wallace felt that when he was speaking to Aria he was truly speaking to Donovan. It was as if the two had fused and Aria was dying to this world a little more each day. And all he could do was stand there, contemplating what might have been.

I don't want to hurt you, Wallace could swear he heard a voice say as he put the first of the boxes down.

The voice was foreboding, yet it had the vaguest intonations of humanity.

You can have a good life ahead of you, the voice continued. *You can find your own bride. Raise your own child. It's not too late for you, yet. If you just walk away. If you just leave me my bride.*

Though Wallace did genuinely sympathize with the ghoul, imagining what it'd be like to wake up to supernatural life without Aria, his sympathies only extended so far. His love, however, extended much farther.

"I won't let you kill her," he felt himself saying to the walls.

She'll awake to a happier life than she'd ever know here, the voice countered.

Wallace gazed over the steps, doors, and walls, searching for something to pin down the elusively resonant voice.

But I warn you, if you stand against our union, if you delay our eternal marriage...

"Do whatever you will," Wallace challenged, slamming down a second box. He cringed, half-expecting to be hurled against a wall.

I understand you, the voice said. *I feel the agony within you: loving a woman who can never truly love you back. Being the ghost in the relationship instead of the husband who's already dead. These thoughts have plagued you.*

"Leave me alone," Wallace insisted, dropping another box. "Be gone from this house, from Aria, from whatever you're doing to her, or I will see you exorcised straight to Hell!"

Again, Wallace braced for physical assault. Again, he was disappointed.

Your pain is as transparent as your threats, as transparent as you are, the voice asserted. *But I respect your love and your pain. If it could've been any other way, if I could've lived without her. If we were not joined eternally, I would've been happy to give you to her to wed. For her sake as much as for yours. You're a good man, Wallace. I wish my adversary wouldn't have been so good.*

But I won't stop; I cannot stop, until she is joined where she belongs, joined to me. I'd beg you to go, for your own safety, out of respect for the feelings Aria has for you, but you won't listen. So I say this to you now in warning before the final day.

"You won't scare me away or fool me as you did that priest," Wallace said, partly for having no threats left to levy.

I knew what you'd decide before you knew, the voice confessed. *For you, it must be until the bitter end. I apologize for what you force me to do, to become. You're a good man. May you stay that way.*

Wallace felt oddly comforted to know that this force, this manipulative evil, did indeed have a conscience, albeit a tortured one. He felt an eerie solace in knowing that another force in the universe had correctly seen his pain, even the depth of his love for Aria, and sympathized. But the sheer disarming of his anger, perhaps the ghoul's true intent, was a vulnerability Wallace could not afford. Love and anger, strange bedfellows though they might have been, were his only convictions at this point, the sole fire fueling him on towards the final showdown, the final battle for Aria's body and soul.

I hate you, Wallace thought, convincing himself of this, *what you've come to be. If you honored your love for her as you claim you do, you'd let her go. You'd let her move on and make her own choices.*

She made her choice before she was ever born, the voice articulated. It ceased momentarily to enjoy Wallace's shock at having his thoughts, his aura, read so easily. *Have a restful night, Wallace. May you die as well as you have lived.*

Wallace muttered—his only defense—and sought to continue unloading the boxes, only to see that, as a last gallant gesture before the war, the ghoul had placed all of the boxes neatly inside. It was clear to Wallace that this was added gall, as if the ghoul had been so certain that Aria would not be Wallace's that he mocked the actual moving process, even allowing the artifacts of his beloved to be relocated to Wallace and Aria's new house. Then it occurred to Wallace: perhaps this suddenly gallant ghoul had simply wanted his opponent fully rested before their mini-Armageddon occurred. Wallace shook his head, feeling a supernatural slumber overtaking him. He slumped over on the steps, still feeling dispossessed, still feeling as if the steps were where he'd always be when it came to Aria.

Bella gulped, watching Aria prancing about the church, in her actual wedding gown, no less, as if she was walking in a mausoleum. While originally Bella had booked the much more lavish St. Anne's Cathedral of West Heights Plains, when Aria called the wedding off, and then on again, this was the only church that still had any openings that came close to the original wedding date. The mother of the bride was particularly tickled that a rehearsal could only be scheduled on the same day as the original wedding, as if to underscore the romantic ambiance of the march down the aisle. But to watch Aria walking, reliving her first wedding, left Bella nothing to do but to stand, masking her humiliation.

"Where's Wallace?" she asked the bride-to-be as the lanky figure of Father McDonald emerged. "It's not like him to be anything but punctual."

"We had a falling out," Aria said matter-of-factly.

"I suppose when someone thinks you're possessed by Satan, that's bound to happen."

"I thought I had you two work that out."

"Working it out became—well—stop talking to each other. I honestly don't know that he'll be here at all."

"You've sold and packed your house, have nearly all your possessions in his custody, and you don't know if the man's going to go through with the wedding?"

Aria advised Bella to take deep breaths.

"I apologize," Father McDonald said upon arrival. He was perhaps the only priest who insisted upon conducting all rehearsals himself, if only to honor the full sanctity of the sacrament of marriage. "This has been a crazy week. With the impending arrival of Rome—."

"Burgundy Hill's become that famous?" Aria asked.

"Its resident ghoul has."

Aria could sense the undercurrent in Father McDonald's reply. Just by looking at the man, she could tell why he took on so sizable an affair as a wedding at so late a juncture. He must've known Donovan to be the mystical tormentor.

Perhaps he felt that marrying the ghost's beloved would trigger something that would help Rome in its holy cause.

"Normally, this is exceptionally short notice for a wedding," Father McDonald went on, as if reading Aria's thoughts. "But with so many couples canceling in light of recent events—"

"I imagine a foul red fog doesn't make for the most romantic backdrop," Aria interjected.

"Time is short, so we need to begin," Father McDonald said. He gazed around, his eyes meeting those of the celestial statues. "Where's the groom?"

"He's been detained," Bella lied.

Normally, such blatant falsehoods hurtled towards a religious would be beyond even Bella, but when it came to her daughter's proper wedding, ethics fell by the wayside.

"I hope it's nothing too serious."

Aria smirked up at the priest. "Potential demonic possession ring a bell?"

Father McDonald shook his stately head. "I will say this—of all the weddings I've presided over, yours are the most. . .memorable."

The smirk gained a playful new life on Aria's lips. She could sense the priest fishing around for anything that might help him in his true cause.

"Your last husband—Donovan, was it?"

"My, you have an impressive memory, Father."

"It was only a little over a year ago, wasn't it? I still remember the man."

"You did preside at his funeral."

"I'd rather it been my own than see young love meet such a tragic end."

The smirk suffered a quick extinction due to the unvarnished honesty of the priest's words. The momentary tone seemed so authentic, so sincere.

"In any event, I'm glad you found new love. Love is nothing if not persistent."

"Thank you, Father," Aria said, fighting not to indulge in thoughts of her last trip down the aisle. "Shall we continue?"

"Without a groom? That determined to become a bride?"

"Nothing will get in the way of my marriage this time."

The dead weight of Aria's words hinted her true intention to the priest. This was not a rehearsal for an earthly wedding so much as for an eternal one. The logic of it escaped the priest, but not the insinuation.

"Perhaps you can start us off, dear. The ceremony hasn't changed all that much in a year," Bella said.

"This time let's go through everything, including the vows," Aria insisted, handing a small piece of paper to the presiding celebrant.

Father McDonald took the scripted vows with reluctance. He had conducted many an exorcism in the farther reaches of the earth, but this, almost the antithesis, was strange new territory for him. Nonetheless, he continued, if only to test his own theory about the hauntings of his parish.

"You'll stay back here," Bella interjected. "Your bridesmaids should be behind you, one with the flowers—that'll be your cousin—and another, your friend, with—"

The crimson candles in the church rose in a great wave of flame, then extinguished. The lighting flared in the fire, then darkened as the aisle chilled.

"Either that's a sign of bad electrical work or a sign from Providence," Father McDonald said. "Either way, we should leave."

"He's here," Aria whispered, starting her wedding march.

Bella's voice grew louder, prattling on even over the supernatural elements.

"Quiet, Mother," Aria insisted as she took her place by the priest. "Father, please take us past the march. Take us through the vows."

"This building is unsafe."

"Father, now!"

"That's ridiculous. I can't have—"

"I can control it. I can calm him." Aria stepped back, turned her dead gaze to the Romanesque ceiling that extended to Heaven itself. "It's okay, my love. Just come to me."

Father McDonald's eyes chased after Aria's all across the ceiling. The lighting did not quiver, nor the shadows from the opalescent light. After a grim moment in the shadows, the elderly priest put a soothing hand on Aria's shoulder, saying simply: "Come, my child."

The scent of burning roses accosted the chapel. Bella, gazing upward, after the source of the smell, stood dumbfounded. Aria and Father McDonald stared quixotically at the old shrew until the snare holding her to her statuesque stance became perfectly visible. In a rainbow of colors, festooning among the awnings in rich ambers, chalky whites, radiant pinks, and bloody magnolias, was a form so nearly human. The eyes, a cobalt to match any ocean, were childlike in their innocent gaze of love. The creature, more light than spirit, kept its eyes trustingly upon its beloved, swirling in constantly changing colors that expressed its vulnerability. This ghost of all seasons, the color of all the roses Aria had ever placed upon its grave, looked for all intents and purposes afraid, deathly afraid, an uncertain groom before a power too great for him to comprehend: the power of a woman.

Father McDonald, surprisingly shaken for such a battle-tested soldier of Christ, started chanting in Latin. The colors began diminishing, the expression of pain deepening in the eyes until Aria put her hand upon the old religious. His words stumbled to a halt. This creature, this Donovan, made haste to rush toward Aria, exploding in a frenzy of haphazard light.

"My baby," Bella exclaimed as Aria collapsed to the floor.

"She's not your baby anymore," Father McDonald corrected her. He placed his hands upon the cooling flesh of the fallen bride. "She's his now. She tricked me," he lamented, thinking of his own stratagem gone wrong. "She's used us both, you and me, to draw him out, to join with him."

"I don't understand. You're a priest. Can't you do something?"

Father McDonald stood over the fallen childlike bride.

"Not by myself. He's proven more powerful, more cunning, than I anticipated. Come. Get her to her bed. I'll get the doctor."

"And if that fails?"

"My brothers should be arriving shortly."

CHAPTER 19:

Antiphon

꩜ Watching the doctors analyze Aria, and come up empty, watching the psychologists taking notes, curiously questioning, with no answers, was more than Bella could bear. Undoubtedly, words like comatose and catatonic—acute schizophrenic complications would find their way on to their blackberries. Bella left them to the analyses that would generate so much fame in academic circles, taking in the inhospitable chill of the hospital lobby.

Don't take her yet, Bella pleaded, thinking of the second lost wedding day. *Not because of my sins.*

Bella would be the first to admit that she wasn't ever in candidacy for mother of the year, that she'd even considered such women failures from a corporate perspective. She was a lawyer seeking a partnership that would earn her more than an appointment to judiciary work ever would. Yet, she found herself thinking of anything but the rights doctors and psychologists had when profiting off of her child. She found herself contemplating motherhood, the great blessing and curse that to her was as mysterious as Creation itself.

In truth, she knew she had approached Aria as she would any other client: donated set hours to her nightly, a lasting appointment from seven to nine. She became furious when the child took more time than allotted, like some selfish divorcee might just to ensure that his ex-wife would be properly vilified before the courts.

I gave her a good life, Bella said in consolation. *Opportunities for a business degree from a second-tier Ivy League school. Dates with eligible young bachelors. A world I never had growing up.*

Secretly, Bella thought of Aria as selfish and ungrateful, as intent to drive her mother to an early grave. Rather than embrace the life Bella so meticulously, so generously, crafted for her, Aria sought to compromise it at every turn. First, there was Donovan. A small pet project of Bella's, a local abused boy who she had unsuccessfully tried to have removed from his drunken father's home. Bella at first admired her daughter's charitable treatment of the child, even encouraged it: that is, until it became clear that Aria wasn't simply being nice.

And when Aria seemingly outgrew him, in the way Bella herself outgrew her men, there were the rumors all about town regarding Aria's less than ladylike contact with many of the local boys. Bella sought to admonish her with the horrid tales of divorcing couples, of the less than respectable marriages she'd be forced to endure if she became pregnant (single motherhood apparently wasn't a concession Bella was willing to make), but got nowhere with the child. Aria just had a mischievous look in her eyes, knowing that soon enough Bella would be summoned back to work, that she could only stay so long.

Motherhood by appointment, that's what I gave her, Bella admitted. *But I had to be my own woman. I had to live my dreams to allow her to live hers.*

The trouble was Aria was more of a free spirit than her mother. She didn't have practical dreams. Everything centered around Donovan. A house, a marriage, children, a job that was only a job, not a vocation. Aria took after her grandmother and was initially, Bella hated to admit, a girly woman, a homemaker, the honorable antithesis of everything Bella's generation had worked so hard to redefine. When Aria majored in business, simply to be able to afford a home away from her mother, Bella was shocked. Her daughter always had a good head for numbers—didn't she know just how many hours, just how many seconds, her mother was late from work each night?—but it wasn't the reason she pursued accounting as a career. It was because accounting paid the bills, helped her live out her dream with Donovan. Always, those dreams came down to Donovan.

And what if he leaves you or you grow tired and leave him? Bella remembered asking Aria one day.

For her efforts, Bella received a resounding slap, one that crackled like thunder over a midnight sky.

We were made for each other, Aria had said, or some such nonsense.

There was no getting anywhere with the child, no matter how much Bella might argue against her first choice of spouse. And so, she attended the wedding and then carefully removed herself from her daughter's life. She never did make partner, but she earned commendable enough settlements to more than pay for an early retirement so that she might finally live.

And for what?

Only to have Aria's father die and to be left without a husband again, Bella thought. *Only to forget what it was that mattered in the first place. A daughter. A family. The people I worked so hard for, who grew so far away from me.*

Not many parents truly felt their children hated them, but Bella was one.

She had it right, Bella had to admit, at least when it came to the miracle of balancing life and career. *She would've done it. She would've had a good job with steady hours and still made enough time nightly for family. My life was wasted*, Bella thought, a little too matter-of-factly. *It was the blueprint she'd work against.*

And in that Bella found renewed purpose—that her own struggles had indeed formed her child's. That her life mistakes had been lessons Aria had learned from. Sure, Bella was proud of her work, of her sacrifices, if not always of her mothering skills. But she was prouder still of her daughter's ability to learn from them.

Please don't take her now, God, she begged in a whisper as the sick and infirm struggled on by. *Please don't let me die until I see her do what I never could: lead a happy, balanced life in a marriage that—miraculously—just might last.*

∾ Wallace dialed Aria's cell and still reached no one.

He called Bella, but even then ate static and static alone.

Wallace had sensed he'd been duped, but he could no longer feel the presence around him, watching him, ensnaring him like some animal of the night. Wallace put down the phone and took up the car keys.

Something awful's happened, he thought. It's not like Bella to avoid a conversation, especially one on marriage.

He drove quickly through gathering fogs that grew so thick they almost impeded the car. Some traces of reddish mist even seemed to have grown ghostly eyes that watched as this transgressor of public fears drove forward without so much as a glance at the specters that had come to rule the town and its weather.

Even among the flitting of spirits, Wallace could no longer feel Donovan's presence. He thought back to the ghoul's last words: I hope you die as well as you have lived. Wallace overlooked the sympathy behind the statement, sensing only insolence and challenge.

Remarkably, not even the fog, the mist, the clouds, rains, or their makers prevented Wallace from arriving at Aria's house. Wallace had half-expected some great challenge from the minions Donovan had gathered to his cause, only to realize that the battle had already been won. The moment he looked at the house, devoid of Aria's Lincoln, he knew: The conquest of Aria was already underway.

Still, Wallace used his key to enter the house, to make sure she was not lying helpless inside. Upon opening the front door, Wallace saw a mess of boxes. So many old items he had carefully packed for The Salvation Army were out, wrinkled, strewn across couch, chair, and floor. It looked to all the world that Aria had nuzzled up against the dark shirts her husband wore, had kept even his ties, vests, and socks. Wallace kept his march, going up the stairs to see if Aria was lying down. Opening up the door to Aria's room, he set eyes on a single artifact adorning the oak bed that Aria had never before let him behold. He saw a black tux—not a rental. It appeared to have been worn—along with dress slacks and shoes—but no Aria. Whatever happened to his fiancée, the message here was clear: Donovan had gained control, and the eternal wedding was at hand.

But where could she be? Wallace asked.

He thought of last night, of the ghostly, dreamless sleep he'd experienced when he should've been at the chapel, assisting the priest in his plan for Aria's spiritual recovery.

That was no rehearsal, Wallace reasoned. *God, may it not be too late.*

Wallace raced down the stairs, nearly slipping on pieces of Donovan's earthly wardrobe, then smelt the unmistakably ashen scent of burning roses. He braced himself, readying himself as much as his mortal self could, when he saw Bella, Father McDonald, and even Aria upon the steps. Bella had obviously been crying. The priest looked more earnest, as if preparing for the battle ahead.

"Where were you last night?" Bella screamed. "We tried to call you. Aria needed you!"

Wallace understood that Bella was screaming at the unfortunate turn in her daughter's fortunes and did not take offense. He struggled with the absurdity of the excuse he had to render, until he finally just released the words to the air.

"This thing—it spoke to me. It kept me away."

Normally, blaming an absence on spiritual tormentors would not be the best in the world of excuses. However, given what Aria looked like right now, her skin pale, purplish even, against a silk white wedding dress, Bella accepted the excuse as easily as if Wallace's car had broken down on the highway and all the world's cabs were simultaneously occupied.

"This spirit—it means to take her here. It has a great deal of emotional currency here. It'll play off Aria's intense reaction to this house and," Wallace added, gazing down, "its artifacts."

Bella turned, looked at the priest for confirmation.

"We'll fight its evil here," Father McDonald said, solemnly. "I don't want this force retreating from the church only to come back and plague the house."

"But it'll have greater power here," Wallace argued.

"Or greater comfort, and less anger, given that it lived with Aria in these surroundings. Either way, you must trust that God's power knows no limits. Bring her to her bed," Father McDonald ordered.

"Father," Wallace protested. "Its wedding tux is on the bed."

"Then the gauntlet has been cast down," Father McDonald said. "The final hour has come."

～ The sickness took color in pale hues, then in flushing rivers of scarlet, all along Aria's thinning face. Though no doctor had successfully explained the rainbow of chromatics, nor even the psychologist, it appeared clear to all who gazed upon her corpselike figure that there was only one answer: This was life's last grand parade before Aria's time came to its unnatural end.

Wallace stood, his face almost mimicking the hues apparent on Aria.

Bella, familiar with the sad mimicry of grief, having lost so many husbands of her own, sought, for once, to offer consolation. "She would've wanted you here," the aging woman added. "I'm glad you made it."

Wallace stood, transfixed in his anxiety. "We just sort of left things uncertain," he eventually whispered. "I just assumed she broke it off—again."

"She needs you to be a husband now," Father McDonald said, "or we will lose her."

"Lose her?"

"To him."

Wallace's stare wandered, seeking out Bella, whose eyes met his, as steadfast as the priest's. "She needs hospitalization," he said.

"Not according to the doctors. They say nothing's wrong—physically," Bella indicated.

"But she's dying."

"My brothers arrive today," Father McDonald added.

Neither Bella nor Wallace spoke.

"Don't abandon hope, Father," Wallace pleaded, his eyes hardening in their black light. "I saw what that monster's capable of. Don't abandon her until it's driven out."

"Can you help her?" Bella asked the priest.

"Only The Lord can. Call me if anything changes. I'll await the bishop's word with prayer and meditation."

～ Had Aria seen her pale, withering frame, barely drawing and receding breath, perhaps she would've put up a fight. Perhaps she would've rallied her flesh before it chilled, awaiting the penultimate kiss that would make her death's bride. Fully arrayed for her eternal union, Aria simply lied there, motionless.

As it was, Aria saw only life—she simply saw it in the form of Donovan. The ghost of rose and fire had taken form, descending down from a golden Heaven, petals fluttering in pointed flame as he reached the figure lying so prone upon the bed. He reached in, scooped up the frightened child's spirit within, lifting her up into the supernatural sky. There, in a striking contrast to the bride-to-be's complexion, thousands of roses, of all hues, all varieties, fluttered in a dancing fire circle around the lovers. Donovan spun Aria through the air as they danced slowly among the roses, as each sensation became conjoined. Aria sensed, in limitless proportions, the immensity of Donovan's love. She could see its iconography all around her, in an entire world of rose-covered oceans, wedding flower petals, rice and confetti, in an eternal feast in which she would perpetually be the guest of greatest honor. This, all that it was, had the warmth of an embrace, the passion of a deep kiss, the depth of a filial bond. This was love, as it was meant to be, in the first light of Creation.

Aria could see no death, no mourners gathered around her final bridal bed. Their cries were lost to the heavenly songs of Donovan's devotion, to the poetry that wrapped itself around her body as assuredly as the rose petals that serenaded her skin even more.

This could be our wedding, Donovan offered with all due enticement, *a wedding that will never end.* The spectral groom appeared, in Aria's vision, more tangible, more human, than ever before, more vulnerable than the white rose manifestation he so favored. He appeared as he once stood, as Aria's fiancé, minutes away from being husband, tall, awkward, possessed and yet not quite possessed by Aria, all at once—the most delicious memory Aria had ever had. There he stood, the man of her life's devotion, offering a ghostly rose of all colors gathering light as he offered it to her like he might a ring.

All you have to do, his voice continued, inside her own consciousness, *is say I do. All you have to do is honor the eternal nature of our marriage.*

Aria could feel her lips nearly speaking the words, but something was not quite right—given the life she had led, Aria knew that marriage was the marrow of life, not the wedding. She pictured the busy hours picking up after children upon returning from analyzing a company's finances all day. The vision Donovan offered had an undeniable girlish appeal to her, but she was a woman, now, far more grown than when they first met, and something unidentifiable about this eternal wedding felt as ghostly as the man before her.

In those few frantic moments of absolute indecision, Aria could hear cries and whispers about her, could almost see shadowy forms covered with a silvery mist of tears. One of those forms sounded almost like Wallace, mumbling. But then, as a priest of some kind chanted, the cries died down and a new spectral image appeared. This manifestation was one of endless reams of raging white fire with eyes of deepest cobalt, a ghost she barely recognized as her beloved, causing a storm of commotion. Pictures of Wallace and Aria, photo journals, mantelpieces, even knives, swirled in a great wind of flame, causing unmitigated shrieking from the shadowy forms that so nearly bathed in their own sanguine red.

Stop, Aria whispered with any strength she might still conjure.

Still, this home, transformed into a shrine, shook as tornado winds clamped down upon it like a smashing fist, startling and shaking the denizens inside. The dresser cracked. Tiny fingers of fire zigzagged over the walls, tearing the paint and plaster behind them. Even the bed shook off the words Bella tried to pour upon them in absolution.

Don't hurt them, Aria barely whispered, scrambling to remove herself from her tomblike bed.

She could see one shadowy figure assume the face, the bereavement, of Wallace, approaching her, clutching her hand, saying something that could not be interpreted, not even as a whisper. Aria's head fell back, as did her body, nearly lifeless.

☙ The hours felt longer in their indecision. It was as if time held Aria, uncertain of quite where to place her. As a loving wife to a new husband? Or as a woman whose last day had just passed?

Bella, keenly aware of her daughter's plight, tried to assume the courage she only wished she had. She could not spend each hour with her daughter, like the more valiant Wallace, who took a leave of absence from work that might very well spell the end of his gainful employment. No, Bella could only remember the precocious child with the face of an angel and the eyes of a devil who enjoyed life and all that it held so much. It was difficult for Bella to watch that joy extinguish with Donovan's death, and more difficult still for her to understand her daughter.

But Bella was a mother and to be a mother once was to be a mother always. And so she stood, started circling the bridal bed, the room, gathering the glass of the broken pictures, using this action as an excuse to step outside.

There, after disposing of the glass, she glanced at any pictures of Donovan as of yet unpacked, something like sympathy seizing her eyes.

"I am sorry," she found herself whispering to the pictures. "I am sorry I stood in the way of you and my daughter. Can't you see that we both wanted what was best for Aria? We just went about it in different ways."

Bella stopped in her soliloquy, half-expecting the graying shadows to answer. She gazed from the pictures to the empty spaces of the living room.

"I feel absolutely ridiculous talking to these walls, but I know you're still alive, somehow, that you're still pursuing her, and I know that you love her. I know you're doing what you feel is best for her. But I'm her mother and I need her too."

Bella broke down, ever so briefly, entirely unaware until this moment of epiphany that motherhood, an enterprise she so looked down upon, meant so much to her.

"You had your day, and I'm so sorry I wasn't there like a mother should've been to welcome you to the family. But I've never said all I had to say. It's too early, always too early, to say goodbye. It's unnatural. It's just not right."

Bella took a picture of the couple, openly kissing it.

"I wish you had lived. I wish you had given her the life I never understood, the life I could only imagine. But for you the hours are gone. Time has slipped away. But not for Aria. You've taught me a lot, Donovan, about who I should've been. Let me teach you something in return. Love is about freedom. It's about letting go. That's the paradox, see. Only in letting go can you hold on to love forever. I'm begging you: Let Aria go. Not just for her mother, but to honor her love."

Bella shook her head at the pictures, the naked foolishness, the futility of her gesture, striking her.

She felt utterly stupid to have an extended monologue with the stirring shadows of the room, yet she knew she had to try. When Wallace emerged, ever so briefly, from holding Aria's hand, Bella sat down and let silence consume her.

"Are you okay?" Wallace asked at last.

"So you heard? Everyone heard, huh?"

Wallace lent Bella a quick smile.

"I had to make the effort. I had to be a mother, at least once," Bella said.

"He won't answer you. Violence is his way."

"He was more than that once. I hope he'll be more than that again before it's too late."

Bella made the pretense of touching up her makeup to cover the quickening tears. Wallace, in a gesture he himself never thought possible, cradled her in his arms.

"You know she admired you, don't you?" Wallace asked. "Once, in the few times she wasn't talking about Donovan, she told me so."

"Nonsense," Bella said, clearly choking on the sentiment she could no longer hide. "It was me who should've admired her, who should've told her so."

"She admired your strength and courage most of all," Wallace offered in consolation.

Bella looked at the man, weighing whether his steady black eyes might carry a lie.

"You're just saying that to keep a broken old woman from crying," Bella reasoned aloud.

"I'm saying it because both Aria and I will need that strength before this is over."

Bella nodded. "I won't let this break you two."

Wallace lightly kissed his mother-in-law-to-be. "Then stay with her now," he said. "I'm going to call the priest and see if he ever plans on getting back here."

CHAPTER 20:

A Ghostly Duet

❧ Aria awoke to find herself in a whole new spectral land. Surrounding her, the endless night sky with its powdery stars just a fingertip away. There she sat, with Donovan, suspended in the air, the crescent moon her chariot. Below her, gardens of rose bushes surrounded her as she saw a ghostly vision of her original wedding day. Looking from outside of time, she was amazed by the radiance of her pink face, easily luminous enough to outshine even the long tress of her wedding gown.

"Where is this?" she asked.

Donovan communicated more with the intensity of his ghostly blue eyes than with words.

This could be Heaven.

"But it isn't."

Not without you.

Aria reached over tenderly, impulsively, for the impossible touch. Beneath the fiery white that became the creature's transparent, wispy arms and head, this Donovan was still a scared little boy. Suddenly aware of his vulnerability, Donovan, with wounded pride, changed the complexion of his ghost land as he sensed himself becoming only an object of pity.

Beneath her, Aria saw an elderly, half-bald man bending near her bed, two adult children, whispering by her, and Aria herself, long since having lost the battle to wrinkles, loose skin, and physical decay. She lay in a stale hospital bed. She could sense this older Wallace tell her that a priest had been summoned.

This will be you, Aria felt Donovan say. *I can save you from that fate. I can give you the wedding you always wanted—one that will never end.*

Aria reached again, unable to feel anything in the ghostly fire that had become her late husband.

"It never ended, not for me," she corrected him.

She reached out to touch the spirit who was himself haunted, only to see the fire of his wrath consume what was his heart in great balls of golden fire.

"Don't you see? A wedding never ends for the bride, not when she's in love. I mean the reality of marriage, the hard work—it all hits and hits hard, but that one moment, that one day—it lives forever. Our wedding never ended. It will live on in me."

Donovan became a storm of spectral fire—his burning arms reaching out, seeking to shake Aria, to make her feel his insurmountable pain.

She could only faintly hear Wallace cry through the deluding light of the ghost land.

"She's, she's—dying?" Bella openly asked.

She'll live on with me, Aria felt Donovan rationalizing.

His grip grew harder, paralyzing, as his touch always was, but this time, in a painful numbness, Aria determined to fight.

Her tiny frame ignited in activity, her arms like tiny wicks igniting the rest of her body into motion. She fought the pressing of mystical arms, the deathly embrace, until Donovan pressed his lips deep onto hers in a kiss that robbed her of all vitality. Aria felt her breathing sputtering, growing more and more sporadic. She could sense a commotion of wails all about her, as her mother and fiancé called her name frantically, sounds she could just make out like the raspy ringing of rusty bells. Still, her pulse slowed, her eyes lost their light, her lips grew in a ghostly blue, unable to articulate so profound an idea as death.

∽ "Welcome, my brother," Father McDonald said in pronouncement. He stood on the slate rectory steps, taking the sole small brown leather case the man from Rome brought.

While leading the man inside, Father McDonald stared at Father Bernito, secretary to the cardinal's office and officiate of Rome's investigating committee upon the rites of exorcism in the Latin church. The black-robed man was large and oblong in shape, like some Friar Tut taken out of legend. Yet, he had the look of an intellectual, still sporting thick-framed glasses that appeared anachronistic in the modern age.

"Where is this woman you told us of?" Father Bernito asked bluntly, with just a trace of an Italian accent.

"She's being watched in her home."

"You released her from your care?" The Italian scholar openly shook his graying head.

"Her mother grew tired of awaiting your arrival. We all can't keep Roman time, Father."

The fat surrounding Father Bernito's cheekbone winced at the naked accusation.

"I assure you this case has Rome's full attention or I wouldn't be here. I've read your letters to the bishop with intrigue. You're convinced this woman is at the source of all of these manifestations?"

"With all due respect to your office, I don't think it's demons we're fighting here, Father, but something far worse—unrequited love."

"We shall see."

Father McDonald placed Father Bernito's case on an adjacent bed.

"Promptly, I hope," the monsignor said, watching Father Bernito unpack. "I knew her, Paulino. I baptized her. I married her to her late husband. And if something isn't done soon, I'll be burying her too."

Father Bernito recorded the monsignor's words duly on the Blackberry he pulled from his case. "You realize we're here merely to investigate, James. The Holy Father himself has an interest in this."

"And has the Holy Pontiff no interest in saving a soul? Paulino, I've said prayers of exorcism to St. Michael. I've fought demons on three different continents. And I can tell you: This ghost, this force, it's going to kill her if we don't act now."

Bernito smiled, if it could be called a smile. It was more an exercise in calculation, a positioning of the lips so that they basked in the man's condescension.

After letting the gesture have its full effect, Paulino Bernito said, "I can see why they placed you here, James. You've truly taken to the locals."

"I'm a priest first, Paulino, not a Vatican man."

"And yet you had such ambition." Father Bernito's green eyes were lost to the gray horizons of time, picturing a youthful vicar of yesteryear that by now even Father McDonald himself had consigned to the ashes of another age.

"Tell me, Secretary, have you ever battled Hell when it seeps out on Earth, taking the form of a child? Have you ever had a demon, a supernatural entity, smarter than you, setting stakes on how to claim your immortal soul?"

Father Bernito coughed, his supercilious smile on the wane as he removed crosses, specialized holy water, and an ancient tome of Latin prayers.

"That cures ambition real fast," Father McDonald said, pausing with what in a less gruff man might've made for piety. "Gives you a new sense of priorities."

"My priorities are His Holiness's, Father," Bernito rejoined. "As yours should be."

Father McDonald felt the disdain of his youth flowing in his blood once again. He had entirely forgotten how much he'd both admired and hated this dowdy intellectual with an ego to match the firmaments. It was then that he prayed to God, that he let the beatitude of the divine engulf his senses before those senses were altogether lost.

"I'm asking for your help, Paulino," Father McDonald said in earnest.

"And yet I've never battled Hell, have I, in the form of a child?"

"You know full well I wrote because I knew they'd send you. I need you because of your expertise in, well, the study of disembodied spirits."

"The Catechism does not—"

"Come now, Paulino. We both know there's more to God's kingdom than any one earthly book of rules can dictate. I know you've devoted your life's work to this. And I know you'll help."

"What makes you so certain? For all I know, this could merely be a case of mass hysteria."

"It's also your chance: the one case with enough media attention to give you the fame you've always sought among Rome's inner circles."

Father Bernito looked up from his emptied case, his green eyes less luminous. "You misjudge me, brother. The glory I seek is not found on earthly realms."

Father McDonald smirked. "Then we shall see if that glory, if God's glory, does truly reach the ends of the earth."

"Do you doubt it?"

"I doubt men. I doubt myself. I doubt everything. It's my nature. Especially when it comes to this one, Paulino. It's more massive than anything I've ever handled. Something simply doesn't feel right, though I can't place my finger on just what it is."

Rather than beam at the confidence Father James McDonald placed in his abilities, Bernito's face drew itself out in suspicion. "I will assist you, Father, but there's still one piece of the puzzle you haven't told me. What is your relationship to this woman?" he wondered aloud. "Why do you speak with such passion?"

"You know very well, Paulino. Even from your chamber in Rome, I'm sure you read and annotated the report."

Bernito said nothing, preferring to let his eyes speak for him.

"I loved her mother, once. But I loved God more."

"Let us hope so."

"Still, when I look at her, I think of what it might've been like had she been my child. Had my family's line continued after me."

"Yet you stayed with the Church."

"I couldn't abandon my people or my God." Father McDonald smiled brusquely. "It's funny. I thought that was my greatest test. But now, here I am again. About to lose this child. Suddenly, I'm not sure which test is greater."

"Have faith, Father," Paulino said in reassurance.

"It's the nature of faith that's the question, Paulino. This is a man's spirit, not a devil's. What, then, does your faith decree?"

"That an evil spirit belongs with his father."

"In Hell?"

"If necessary. It is for God Almighty to decide. All we know is that he does not belong here, and it is our divinely appointed role to drive it out."

"If only he knew where he belonged. If only any of us did."

"Then we'd both be out of work, wouldn't we, Father?"

Father McDonald's lips rose into a reluctant smile.

"Get some rest, Paulino. It may be the last peaceful night either of us ever sees."

The land of ghostly delights, past a sun sitting in a garden bed of stars, called out to Aria in all its celestial bliss as Donovan approached her again for the first time. No more a ghoul, he was just as she preferred to picture him, standing in a wrinkled tux on the happiest day of her life.

My lady, Donovan offered, outstretching his hand.

Aria reached out, hesitant that the absence of touch might make this all a dream soon lost to night. She remembered the last time Donovan appeared before her, where the two worlds of flesh and spirit stood in the way of contact.

I can touch you here, Aria said. She smiled as she had when Donovan first carried her home, bruised and cut, from the shore, when they were children, so many ages ago. *I can actually feel you here.*

Donovan's face took on a boyish smile of its own. *This is our little pocket of eternity,* he insisted. *Our wedding will never end.*

Aria smirked at the thought. While romantic, her earthly wedding day was incredibly chaotic, full of panicking over last-minute touches of makeup, over relatives bickering, over every minor detail. It held a beautiful anxiety, but not one she wanted to carry into eternity.

Sensing this, Donovan created a garden of roses that stretched out, like stars, all across the sky.

Aria giggled girlishly, taken by the beauty of so many new colors she'd never seen before. She wanted to run through, become each of those colors, reach out and touch every last flowery star.

Catering to her whims, Donovan took her in his arms, and together they ascended and spun across the sky. Falling rose petals cascaded across Aria's body, each one as warm as Donovan's love. They were red, white, pink, purple, and gold, a collective of colors she hadn't even imagined. The petals chimed together as they collided, first sounding like silver bells at Christmas, then like some Pachelbel's canon of the Heavens as they circled to a heavenly altar in the shape of the sun.

We can marry here forever, Donovan told her. *Our vows will never grow old. Nothing, not even death, will separate us. If you only say that you will.*

Aria gazed at her mystical groom, lavished in the falling of the rose petals all across the sky.

Nothing would make me happier, she confessed. *If only it were so.*

Yet something felt out of place, even in eternity. She stared into Donovan, seeing the debonair young man she'd so fallen in love with every day of her mortal life.

Yet, the storm-filled eyes held something else, something that was not at peace, even with her in his arms. There was rage, anger, aggression, feelings she remembered from his mortal counterpart, feelings that had only magnified in her absence. She looked deeply into those blue orbs, asking herself if she ever truly knew him, if she even knew him now.

I am our love, Donovan said not through words, but through touch.

Aria caressed the light that made up his cheek, his hair, his hands, soothing him, until another part of her heart called from the earth below. Amid all the chiming petals, she heard the echo of a voice, faint as a child's, that leapt up and caught the crook of her ear. She could hear, but not yet visualize, the breaking voice, the bending legs, the collapsing frame of the man she was to call husband, as he took to his knees, in absolute ruin.

Donovan fought to keep the ruined man's voice mired in a shadowy silence, but the urgency of the emotion, equal to that energy that became his ghostly life, could not be so easily cast aside.

But I love her, a voice from the other world called out. It struck Aria in its own helpless simplicity. *I do love her. I'd give my life for hers.*

Even Donovan could no longer hide the truth. Aria could hear the jolt that, like the thunder of a thousand ages all riled together, gave her flesh new animation. She could see the trembling little man for what he was: deeply in love and deeply sincere. His pale flesh quaked in trickling lines of agony that puddled together, only to cut sharply across his face, then sink, awash in the sudden warmth of tears. There he knelt, as if paying homage to a fallen idol, his face collapsing in worn brown hands, his body convulsing in shameful revelation.

Aria looked back into Donovan, imploring.

Our Heaven would be his Hell, she thought. *I can't let him suffer so. I do love him.*

The naked confession of her thoughts, felt by Donovan in the otherwise inexplicable waning of her touch, struck a violent chord of endless anger within him. As his true form, swirling sables, reds, and ambers of endless storm, re-emerged, she could feel the wound smarting in violent frenzies of light emanating from him.

You don't know what you're saying, Donovan's thoughts insisted. How eager he seemed to dismiss so blatant a breach in their eternal accord. *You're mine. You made the vow. You are my wife. You are me.*

Please, Aria pleaded. *Don't make this harder than it already is.*

I won't let you suffer the ignominy of death. I won't let him seduce you. I won't let you fall into mortal decay, Donovan rationalized. His colors mounted in anger at every word.

A frenzy of storm clouds seized the skies, tearing them with reams of lightning and filling them, through the red fog, with a stench of endless decay. The windows of Aria's room smashed, letting in the bullets of rain. The furniture shook as the walls shook in the pain of Donovan's cries, until Aria, forcing herself up, into consciousness, felt a supernatural stranglehold upon her neck and body. She could see the rose petals circling around her, taking on the violence of Donovan's words. This ghost grew so loud in its fury that it prevented Aria from hearing Wallace's cries as he approached the bed. The wails, hisses, curses, and screams grew louder still, so that Aria could not hear the full fear of her mother's screams as Aria nearly fainted.

With that, Wallace and Bella could've sworn they heard a banshee-like wail, followed by *She's mine* emanating from Aria's own lips. Those lips and skin grew purple as some entity, not seen but felt, pinned her to the marriage bed that might shortly become a deathbed as well.

"I'll call the priest," Bella muttered. She fled the room as Wallace knelt by his fiancé, determined to see out the storm.

"No need," Wallace called out, seeing the widening eyes of men in the street below. "This thing's practically inviting them in."

༄ "Did I just hear windows smashing up above?" Father Bernito asked by way of introduction.

"Welcome to Hell, Father," Bella said in accusation. "So kind of you two to remember your jobs."

Father McDonald, perhaps too moved by the motherly fear that consumed his one-time fiancée, walked up and abruptly kissed Bella on the forehead.

"I'm sorry, Bella," he said. "I simply had to see Father Bernito here. It seems Rome itself has taken an interest and he's the best there is when it comes to dealing with the supernatural."

Bella pushed the firm shoulders of the parish priest away. "My daughter's up there, suffering, calling out in strange voices that he won't let her go, and you're worried about appeasing Rome? I thought you were more of a man than that, James."

Father McDonald's face sank, wrinkles and all. "What I'm telling you is that I can't rid this Donovan on my own or I would've, Bella. With Father Bernito here, we might just stand a chance."

Bella turned back to the stairs. "And why is that?"

"He may've seen fewer cases, but he's never lost one yet."

Intrigued, Bella observed the overbearing man, with his tidy leather case and spectacles that appealed to implore for reason in a senseless world.

"I've seen spirits controlling the winds," Father Bernito began, "exorcised a demonic chorus that jointly possessed three young women, and studied ghostly texts from nearly every sect of Christianity."

"Then I've seen worse than you," Bella said, briefly smirking. She again turned her attention to the task of surmounting the stairs.

Madam," Father Bernito called after her, "you realize the ambitious nature of my task, do you not? I am here to help your daughter, but my primary mission is to save this town."

"Paulino!"

"She has a right to know, James," Father Bernito said, blankly.

"Just what are you saying, Father?" Bella asked.

"That you should know, as James has already intimated, that not all of those possessed survive the exorcism. Sometimes the victim is lost and sometimes the priest."

"I think I'm comfortable risking the priest," Bella said, her smirk now fully in control of her lips.

"But are you comfortable risking your daughter?"

Bella said nothing, just stood, her hand on a rail, halfway up the stairs.

"You must decide before I see her," Father Bernito insisted. He cast a disapproving glance upon his fellow religious. "I really thought James would've told you this, would've had you sign off on the necessary papers."

"Of all the times, Paulino!" Father McDonald called out.

"My daughter's nearly in Hell and you want me to sign papers?" Bella hollered down the stairs.

"You must, madam," Father Bernito insisted. "You must also produce written evidence from doctors and psychologists. Evidence that she's been analyzed fully. Upon my approval, we can then proceed."

"You and your church," Bella stammered, marching back down the stairs. "See what you left me for, James? Are you happy you signed on?"

"I'll see to Aria," Father McDonald said by way of answering.

"You may not exorcise until I say so," Father Bernito called after the parish priest.

Father McDonald responded by muttering incoherently along the length of the stairs.

"You living alone for the rest of your life, that I can see," Bella said to Father Bernito.

She raised a pen, all too willing to sign her legal rights away.

Chapter 21:

Codetta

～ For days Aria lie there, her skin losing more of its luster until it became a thin blue veil separating her from the next world. Her breathing grew more erratic, to the point where it was nearly impossible for attending physicians to determine if she was breathing at all. Only when she was about to be transported to a hospital for extensive care did Donovan allow her to draw breath regularly again, to regain just enough health for the doctors to once again dismiss the threat to her life. And just what was Wallace to say? That a supernatural entity sucked away the very animus of Aria? That it was all a ploy to make Aria its bride in the next world just as she had been in this one?

It was only when Bella insisted on seeking other means of ridding Aria of this monster, as she put it, that Donovan grew frantic and frightful. Unholy smoke covered the room, driving the two mortals out. Only then could his spirit cradle his beloved, seeking her assurance, her protection, even from the words she had last spoke—a jilting Donovan could hardly believe had come so adamantly from Aria's lips.

Didn't Aria see the scenes of us as children? the ghoul thought. *Didn't she see the times we first held each other on the shores? Didn't she see all the visions of the past I sent her from the grave?*

As always, silence alone accompanied his thoughts.

What more can I do? Donovan wondered. *Were promises not made? Were we not sworn to each other for eternity?*

Aria's words and thoughts came back to him. *I love him,* she had said.

The ghostly suitor repeated the words, every subtle intonation, to himself, but could come no closer to believing them.

Yet, Donovan feared the prospect of eternal separation so much so that he'd rather cast himself in flames than face an eternity without Aria. At present, he knew that victory might assuredly be his. With one burst of supernatural fire, he might permanently remove Aria from her corporeal limitations. Yet, he panicked at the thought.

I love her too much for that, Donovan realized.

He thought back across the ages they shared together: *Was that not love? Who knows her like I know her? Who can love her like me?*

And yet, Donovan couldn't bring himself to answer the question. In the year since his passing, Aria had undergone a metamorphosis of her own. No bright streams of rose and fire signaled her change, but change she did, into a stronger, more independent woman. It wasn't that Donovan feared this. In fact, he encouraged it. But the change was not without casualties, and one such casualty was the symbiotic nature of their love.

Was it love at all? Or simply limerance? Or maybe just obsession or infatuation?

The thoughts were cruel ones, cold ones Donovan could not bring himself to fully contemplate. *We are bashert,* he would insist to himself. *We are chosen for one another.*

Even those thoughts grew hollow, cold.

Please, Donovan said, looking down upon the face he so loved in life and even more in death. *Don't leave me to face eternity alone. It's not the way it was meant to be. It's not eternity without you.*

The face, still with some hint of girlishness from their seasons on the shores, still with the slight blush of a rose across the cheeks, held Donovan's rapture. But the thoughts would not relinquish his fears.

You do love me; you do need to be with me, don't you? I won't abandon you. I won't leave you to the coldness of the world, he vowed.

Aria, so close to death, slumbered now, her consciousness caught between two worlds. Enraged as he was, Donovan simply couldn't bring himself to kill her, preferring her to pass of her own initiative. And so, with no answer and no solace, Donovan simply cradled Aria for days at a time, seeking a simpler memory when all he had to do was hold her, when there were no grandiose machinations like death at work in the world.

I'll win your whole love back yet, Donovan vowed with boyish purity. *In honor of you, I'll paint our love across the sky.*

⤫ "Are you ready, James?" Father Bernito called in to the kneeling statue of a man.

Father McDonald was the very tableau of torment. The grayish skin of his upraised hands clasped together so fervently as to draw blood upon his black robe.

"The doctors have returned word, then?" Father McDonald asked without rising to his feet. "The paperwork is done, I take it?"

"According to her mother's records, she's seen two hospitals, four physicians, and three psychologists," Father Bernito said, reading from his Blackberry. "No natural causes can be determined, though one psychologist is still toying with the idea of some rare type of schizophrenia."

"Does The Holy Father know?"

"He's left it in the hands of your bishop." Father Bernito handed Father McDonald a letter with an official seal. "His Excellency has given us permission to investigate and, if necessary, commence."

Father McDonald read the letter, then caught Father Bernito's eye.

"Paulino, I'll do whatever in The Lord's will must be done. But I don't want to put you in harm's way, so let me be direct. I've been praying for three days now. I honestly don't know if I have the strength to live through another one of these."

"Now's not the time to doubt, James."

"Then I wish there were an appointed time, my brother. Didn't Ecclesiastes speak of a time for every purpose under Heaven?"

"Everything under Heaven, James—not everything come up from Hell."

Father McDonald searched around again for the wandering eye of his co-exorcist. "Don't be too quick to label this a demon."

"Whatever's brought the ghostly ravages and this dismal red fog that chokes me half to death is surely not a man."

"A man is many things, Paulino. There is more than is dreamt of in your philosophy."

Paulino smirked. "You've changed."

Father McDonald thought back briefly to his more carefree days of study in the seminary. He remembered the ambitious Paulino, even then burying his nose in some ancient ecumenical text. "Men have changed me," Father McDonald confessed. "Don't give up on Man just yet, my brother. Not even God has done so."

"Nor the devil, so far as I can tell."

Father McDonald helped Father Bernito gather the tools of his trade, from holy water and scriptural dicta to crucifixes and invocations.

"What's her Christian name?" Father Bernito asked as he carried his case to the car.

"Aria Elizabeth," Father McDonald replied softly.

"Why do you ask? She's not the one we're trying to exorcise, my brother, but whatever it is that's inside her. Don't tell me you're getting sentimental on me now, Paulino."

"You're too hard on me, my brother. The years find us changed men."

"This night will find us changed too."

"So tell me, what was she like, this Aria of yours?"

Father McDonald smirked. Too much of the world was in that smirk. "She was like a daughter," he replied, opening the car door for Father Bernito. "She never knew. . .just how close she came to being that daughter. After tonight, she never will."

⎨⎬ The red fog of the dead was not the only supernatural element coloring the climate of Burgundy Hill.

175

At the thought of Aria's prolonged absence from his touch, Donovan painted himself across the canvas of sky, which itself became a storm of seven colors: like the roses once laid so carefully upon Donovan's grave, each season of their love was made manifest. The wrath of red, tempered by the purity of white, the friendship of yellow, the tender beauty of pink. All spoke of the mortal love that had outlived even the ages, becoming eternal. Indeed, the whole sky filled with the specters of falling roses, as a storm of short and long-stemmed roses alike descended upon Aria's house, upon all the township.

"Have you ever seen the like?" Bella asked Wallace. She stared upon the showers upon showers of roses descending to the earthly plain below. "Remarkable."

"He truly loves her," Wallace calculated, a hint of vulnerability filling the air.

Bella grabbed Wallace by the shoulders. "It's his way of seducing her," she said. "Wallace, you must be strong during all of this, as you asked me to be strong. You must be steady in your love, or we will lose her."

"The priests are ready."

"If you don't open yourself, if you don't give yourself over to your love of her, all will be lost."

Wallace shook his weary black head. How much older he felt, this man of thirty-five. "Some good that did me earlier," he said. "Groveling like a child over a bride who'd be just as happy to be dead."

"I saw her move. I saw her struggle for a moment against this, this thing that holds her."

"I would've made a good husband," Wallace lamented. "I would've made an even better father."

Bella slapped Wallace hard enough to strike bone. The gesture, louder than the cracking of flame on oak, roused him. Still, he stared vacantly, a victim of his own thoughts.

"You will be a good husband, if you can act like one now! She needs a man, Wallace, not a child, which is what this monstrous entity is, in its own way."

Wallace simply stared out at the unending sky.

"But how? How to fight such a power as their love?"

"Stay by her, even when the priests arrive. Let her know you'll never leave her side. That's love, Wallace, not a shower of roses."

Wallace nodded, first weakly, then with renewing confidence.

"The time for me to be a mother is now, Wallace," Bella said, tightening her stance, "just as the time for you to be husband is at hand. We may not have been there for her always, Wallace, but between the two of us we'll make Hell pay."

At this, the storm of so many colors grew violent, unleashing shards of hail along with howls, cries, and curses, all wrapped in unrelenting winds. The rain itself became as blood, covering the falling roses until not one was free of the blood of the marriage that was murdered one year ago.

"Take her hand," Bella ordered.

Wallace complied, his features, so stern, softening ever so slightly at the recollection of what it felt like to hold this hand for the first time.

The roses fell, the winds raged, the hail flew, but still Wallace knelt, holding that hand.

◯ Donovan felt a keen shock when he saw Wallace welcome the priests in with all the diligence he might've shown an emissary of the world of commerce. The effect was not lost on Father McDonald, a saint of a man who, on a typical Sunday, devoted himself to the conversion of just such a sinner—the average man of the business world too devoted to Mammon, too devoid of the business of God. But today was no Sunday, no ordinary day of devotion. Today the eternal battle between Heaven and Hell showcased itself in the demure body of an accountant who lay on her bed, slumbering, each second growing more and more pale as some indiscernible power gained on her.

"We've contacted the leading psychologists at the University of Windham," Wallace prattled on. "They're at a loss to explain it."

"We know," the parish priest interrupted, patting Wallace's shoulder. "Stay by your wife."

Father Bernito came in, case in hand. Father McDonald turned to Bella; his face was not full of approbation, but of mercy. He touched her on the shoulder, not gently, but securely, meeting her eyes so that she knew that he, as much as a man could, understood.

"You realize I'm simply here to observe the afflicted, to make a recommendation for his grace, the bishop," Father Bernito asserted.

Bella's dark eyes hardened.

Father McDonald could sense the verbal lashing that would ensue. "We'll do whatever we can," he said in correction. "We'll not abandon your daughter."

The situation was indeed most peculiar. Aria didn't appear to be in pain, so much as in eternal slumber, her body rising and falling in only the faintest whispers of life. Even her hair, spreading out in small waves of black from the sun of her face, made her look cared for, tended—hardly kept by the powers of Hell. Still, for all the momentary serenity, Father McDonald sensed a presence, believed someone, something hovered, observing him meticulously. He could even feel a small pressure in his chest as he approached the afflicted woman to ascertain just how much life she still had in her.

"How long has she been like this?" Father Bernito asked.

"Nearly two weeks," Wallace told him. "We've sought the best medical professionals this side of the Atlantic. All are baffled—there just doesn't seem to be anything wrong."

A word broke through the barrier of Bella's lips, took to the air, then fell into silence.

"What was that?" Father McDonald asked.

"She has been. . .rather depressed," Bella said.

Wallace winced.

"She's planning a wedding and she missed him, it, her former husband, terribly," Bella prattled on.

"Her husband was the man I buried over a year ago. Don't be thick-headed, Paulino—we've discussed this before. Let's just get to it already."

"An accurate account must be made," Father Bernito reasoned.

"She's never forgotten him," Bella added, her eyes darting from her child to the walls. "He hasn't forgotten about her, either."

"I see," Father Bernito replied. "Apparently, his soul cannot find peace."

"He was never at peace, Father," Bella said, "not from the time he was a little boy."

The priests took out all the elements necessary for a blessing: holy water, a Bible, a crucifix, but even they shook at the ghoul's wavering touch, almost taking on lives of their own. Father McDonald, a hardened skeptic cast, ironically, in the role of a penultimate believer in the divine, felt his skin tense as he wondered whether this might be a better-natured spirit than he originally thought. The Bible flew from his hands, opening unto Christ's words about man leaving his mother and clinging to his wife, upon St. Paul's famous treatise of love, then upon the Pharisees questioning Jesus upon the wife with many husbands, then upon Jesus speaking of adultery of the mind. When the Bible closed thunderously, and a cry of agony replaced its presence in the air, the priest took out another case, this one with ancient Latin scrolls and more powerful incantations.

"He's not a demon, Father," Wallace, still pragmatic, asserted. "Aria wouldn't want you to hurt him."

Bella's eyes struck like the fangs of a startled viper, using Wallace's moment of quiet vulnerability to full advantage.

"Do whatever you have to do to save my baby," Bella ordered, keeping her eyes on Wallace, "and his wife."

Wallace, defeated by the mention of a single word, nodded weakly.

"I've dealt with this kind of spirit before," Father Bernito noted. "He may not be demonic, but that doesn't mean he's of Christ."

"If there is good in him, Christ help us to find it," Father McDonald prayed quietly.

The elderly priest felt the eyes of something supernatural upon him. His skin grew frigid. The limp hairs on his arms and legs stood up stiffly, creating a tiny blanket of fear. Still, he refused to give the ghoul any ground. He simply stared down each part of the room, from the mahogany dresser to the oak bed frame, before approaching the slumbering bride. How deathly her features looked.

How helpless the old minister felt in the face of so unassailable a foe. He sensed the ghost feeding on his negative energy. The fear, the uncertainty, the anger, all took almost corporeal form not only in him, but in this spectral creature that so meticulously studied him. Even so, the priest proceeded, undisturbed, until he placed a hand on Aria's wet forehead.

It was at that point that the room again became an epicenter of a preternatural storm. Fresh lightning unleashed its frenzy upon the walls while dressers and stands levitated, only to come crashing down upon each other in a massive quake of activity. Clearly, the ghost was united to Aria in the most fundamental aspects of existence. Father McDonald thought the strange force might truly be energy latent in Aria herself, until he called the ghost by its name.

The power of the summons became a force not even Father McDonald anticipated, unleashing Donovan's cunning over the natural world for all to see. This time, Donovan became the sky, and with it, another color of love. The raging red of the bloody roses transformed into a glistening white, the purity of snow, as a processional of wind and snowflake transformed into spectral scenes of a wedding eternal.

Over the canvas of fallen roses, the snowflakes, each in decorative majesty, held sway over the skies, each enlarging to become a scene of the innocence of first love. One spectral procession showed a youthful Donovan and Aria touching baby fingers; another, the words Aria comforted Donovan with on the night she discovered his father abused him. The processions worked their way up to the aisle where Donovan and Aria first proclaimed their vows for the ages. Each procession of snowflakes was a lasting testimony to the strength and endurance of love in its purest form.

Father McDonald stared outside, baffled at the veracity of what he was seeing. Even Father Bernito dropped his case. Only Wallace held firm, gripping Aria's hand, and even he had to look away. How hard it was to view this as a demonic spirit or vengeful ghost. The allure of the purity of love seduced them as well, until Father McDonald pulled them away.

"Even the darkness can create the light," Father Bernito reminded him. "These majesties are mere illusion."

Bella stared, openly weeping as she saw how much the moments Donovan shared with her daughter meant to him.

This was, after all, her only baby, and reliving Aria's life, so close to her impending death, was too much for even the hardened hater of men to take.

Before Father McDonald could guide her eyes from the window revelations, Bella saw the roses line up, forming a spectral altar. She saw the images in the snowflakes line the aisles as Donovan so clearly called Aria forward. Everything was arranged so beautifully. There was nothing of evil in it. Then Bella reminded herself that this wedding was merely a euphemism for death, that Donovan was indeed struggling to get Aria to willingly give up the body.

"Close the shades," she screamed out, taking Aria's other hand, opposite Wallace.

Father Bernito quickly complied, only to feel the wind throwing him back into the room, only to see the processional of pictures grow larger as the falling flakes chimed out musical notes of love.

As the wind lashed out, striking Father McDonald down alongside his Vatican counterpart, Bella could swear she felt a grip in Aria's hands. Bella's eyes rose and met Wallace's. Just then, Bella felt Aria stir, but the eyes, their coldness, their perpetual winter stare, were not ones she recognized as her daughter's.

"We will be together for eternity; we are *bashert*; we are fated," the purplish lips articulated before the body again dropped down, and the grip vanished.

Weakened by her daughter's seeming preference for death, Bella let go of her hand and backed up into the processional winds.

"It's not her," Wallace called out. "It's him."

"It is," Father McDonald confirmed, rising. "You two must leave now—for your own lives."

"I will not abandon my daughter," Bella called out.

By now her eyes were rivulets of water, blemishing her mascara.

Father McDonald turned to Wallace. A final plea lit the corners of his gray eyes.

"I won't leave my wife," Wallace asserted.

"He's drawing from your emotions," Father Bernito said. "Eventually, he will kill you if necessary. We will draw him from her body, by rites of exorcism if necessary. But you must trust us. You must go."

"I'd give my life for hers," Wallace insisted, gripping Aria's hand tighter. "Say your rites."

CHAPTER 22:

The Final Movement

The Latin rites were minutely particular as to the removal of a demon, and even as ocher storm clouds gathered around Aria's bed, Father Bernito saw strictly to their observance.

After making the sign of the cross, and enjoining all present to do likewise, he, along with Father McDonald, sprinkled the afflicted, all present, the bed, even the chamber, with holy water. The two priests knelt down, one at each side of Aria. Wallace and Bella took opposite sides, having refused, despite the priests' objections, to relinquish Aria's hands.

"Lord, have mercy," the priests called out, signaling to Wallace and Bella to repeat the prayers. "God, the Father in Heaven," they began, awaiting Wallace and Bella, "have mercy on us."

"God, the Son, Redeemer of the world," they continued, until Wallace and Bella said again, "have mercy on us."

As they continued the litany of the saints, the bed did not shake. Strange curses of ancient tongues did not sprinkle the air. No, save for the warning of thunder and cloud all around Aria, Donovan was quiet, pressing his spirit into Aria's, bunkering down to avoid all removal.

The invocations continued, frequently commencing with "Deliver us, O Lord" and carrying on, in litany fashion, with "From all sin" or "From your wrath." Still, the spirit did not seem agitated.

Instead, the scent of the yellow rose took to the air as a new storm of rose petals took Burgundy Hill. The more the entity clung to Aria, the more he authored visions of the endless times she abandoned him. Images of Aria diving into the arms of countless teen lovers during their youngest days filled her, along with images of each time she took solace in the arms of Wallace in the days since Donovan's passing. Images of Donovan standing in the snow, waiting for Aria to come out from school, of driving her back and forth to college classes, of him waiting, enduring all, to stand by her, serenaded the air.

"He's convincing her he's no harm to her," Father McDonald said plainly.

"Do not deviate now, Father," Bernito said. "Now is when the enemy will trick us with his visions."

But Donovan did not need trickery when he had sincerity on his side. He simply turned the litany to the saints into a litany to Aria.

Let me deliver you, Love, from all pain.

Let me deliver you, Love, from this separation, from all the world's callous intrusions.

Let me deliver you, Love, from this illusion of a life.

Those attendant upon the slumbering bride could hear the voice, but not place its presence. Eyes circled, but did not land.

Father McDonald signaled Father Bernito with a flick of his forefinger.

"We must continue, brother," Father Bernito admonished.

"Our words are only helping him."

Donovan continued in his own incantations, delivering a litany just for Aria.

The first among all women, hear me.

Vessel of all beauty, hear my prayer.

Ark of joy, hear me.

Rose of all roses, hear my prayer.

Woman I first touched, hear me.

Keeper of my soul, hear my prayer.

The rose petals flourished with each line the ghost uttered, until even the incantations of the priests could not be drowned out.

"He's professing his love to her," Bella shouted over the litany.

Father McDonald caught Father Bernito's eyes. "This is no demon."

"Even demons have mastery over the human heart," Father Bernito replied. "You of all old priests should know not to trust the senses. They're being used against you!"

"Father, we must regroup," Father McDonald called over the storm of roses.

"Every moment we delay brings the child closer to damnation," Father Bernito hollered in return. "Stand firm!"

"Do not keep in mind, O Lord, our offenses or those of our parents, nor take vengeance on our sins," Father McDonald resumed.

Father Bernito led a rendition of The Lord's Prayer with all in assembly, during which a new storm formed and intensified, the clouds covering the room in a supernatural mist of gold.

"God, by your name save me," Father McDonald called out, alternating at precise intervals with Father Bernito and all in attendance. "By your might defend my cause. God, hear my prayer; hearken to the words of my mouth. For haughty men have risen up against me, and fierce men seek my life; they set not God before their eyes. See, God is my helper; the Lord sustains my life. Turn back the evil upon my foes; in your faithfulness destroy them. Freely will I offer you sacrifice; I will praise your name, Lord, for its goodness, Because from all distress you have rescued me, and my eyes look down upon—"

The golden mist stifled the priestly voices, silencing those in attendance.

Aria, by your love, save me, the ghostly entity said, adapting the famous psalm. *By the love that defends my cause. God, hear my prayer; hearken to the words of my mouth. For haughty men have risen up against me, and fierce men seek my wife; they set not God before their eyes. See, God is my helper; the Lord sustains my life and my wife. Turn back evil upon my foes—*

"Enough! Be silent, you manifestation of Hell," Father Bernito chastised. "Do not speak the words of The Lord!"

The darkening mist filled the nostrils of all present with the stench of death, burning at them with nauseous fumes of sulfur. Bella guided a weakening Wallace to the door, and even Father McDonald fought to pull a fainting Father Bernito from the premises.

"You should've left me," Father Bernito cried out as the door to the bedroom shut after them. "We'll now have to face the demon at his full strength."

"So long as you're at yours," Father McDonald said. "This is no demon. This is something else entirely, and I fear there's not so much as a line in those books of yours to prepare us for him."

∽ Even the entity could not deny it. The more time Aria's spirit spent in the land between the living and the dead, the more attuned her supernatural senses became.

Donovan attempted to console her with a spiritual baby, perhaps one of the ghouls over whom he gained dominion in resurrected form. Donovan gave Aria the life, in brief flickers of eternity, that he so longed to give her in the corporeal form. The house, the furniture, even the angle of the amber sun as it hit the windows—everything was as Aria remembered it to be in their first days together as man and wife. Aria felt love like a wind, like a physical as much as a spiritual sensation, wrapped all around her. Still, as much comfort as she took from the mere presence of her beloved's aura, the senses that came with her disembodied spirit kept tingling, kept signaling her that something wasn't quite right. She let the baby vanish and turned to Donovan.

It's not illusion, Donovan communicated, with feeling rather than with word.

Donovan took to the practice of weaving in and out of Aria. One of the great joys Aria discovered in the spirit was that any soul could join with any other soul in an ecstasy of creation. She sensed her dead husband was using this to seduce her to the other side, to comfort her as her body wasted away. Yet, she could not succumb to its power.

Not illusion? Did I ever really know you? Aria thought, simply. *The murders, the injuries to others, the obsession. I never knew that side of you.*

Death is the illusion. Anything I've done to others has no eternal consequence.

The thoughts flowed freely now, one into the other, so that Aria could not tell where her thoughts ended and Donovan's began.

It has meaning to the lives you hurt.

If they just stayed away, if they just let us be what we are, husband and wife, they would've lived.

And what of you? What of this life? I loved you, Donovan. I won't ever forget you! I can't stand to see you so miserable! You're my Heaven. . .and my Hell.

I can't control what I'm becoming. I swore to live on as our love. This is that love.

This isn't love. It's something. . .darker. And whatever it is, it isn't you.

It's more than me. It's us. I sacrificed so much of my immortal life for you and I'd sacrifice it again willingly. This is the one place in eternity I built for us, the one kingdom we can occupy, away from them, away from their endless interferences, where we could just exist as our love. But they won't let us. They won't stop intruding. I won't let them stop our eternal wedding. They must be dealt with.

Please, don't, Aria importuned, already sensing the thought that lurked on Donovan's spectral mind.

There is only one other way: forget Wallace. Be my bride for eternity. Swear to me here and now.

I. . .I love you so much, Aria replied, thinking of a real life, or a real baby, with her new beloved. *But I can't. Please. I just can't.*

Through the divided consciousness Donovan could not hide, she saw the storm engulfing the priests as they bickered about how best to approach the entity.

"It's the worst case of willful possession I've ever seen," Father McDonald could be heard saying.

"Willful? You've been fooled by this monster," Father Bernito reasoned.

"I tell you she is a willing hostage and casting this misguided soul out may kill them both."

"Then why would this entity fight us every step of the way? Why would he not invite us to continue?"

"Hasn't he? He's prideful beyond question. But haven't his storms allowed us to proceed each time? Hasn't he allowed us to bring his wife to him?"

The idea that Donovan would willfully murder his own love was too much for the spirit to bear. The fumes that had gathered from the cemetery wafted across from the bed, out underneath the door, assailing the nostrils and lungs of the two religious.

Donovan, please—they'll die!

They'll merely pass on to eternity.
I beg you!
Give me your hand.
I can't. I swore to Wallace. I love Wallace too.
Give me your hand and end this.

How quickly Aria saw the fire conjuring itself in the opaque blue eyes. How quickly she saw this creature losing more and more of his humanity by the day as the eternities opened up before him. This wonderful day of a family being born, and wedded, had now come down to what Donovan always seemed to bring with him: death and more death. She reached out her hand and in that gesture offered her life.

All too happy to oblige, Donovan reached out in ghoulish ecstasy as his minion ghosts chimed unholy bells from some shadowy netherworld shrine. Donovan almost sealed eternity with a kiss as the two priests, having been released, according to the ghost's honor, started chanting again. The entity felt his love shuddering in his arms, shrinking away.

Donovan unleashed his wrath upon the priests, who by now had made it far enough in their ritual to cry out to God: "Holy Lord, almighty Father, everlasting God and Father of our Lord Jesus Christ, who once and for all consigned that fallen and apostate tyrant to the flames of Hell, who sent your only-begotten Son into the world to crush that roaring lion; hasten to our call for help and snatch from ruination and from the clutches of the noonday devil this human being made in your image and likeness. Strike terror, Lord—"

That last line, so passionately presented to the Heavens, was all that Donovan needed to hear. He conjured another storm, a fifth and deadly storm eclipsing the storm of mist. He summoned all the ghouls and lost souls he had dominated in the days since his death to wreak havoc upon the room and all therein, save Aria. The skies of Burgundy Hill filled with a rain of ghosts as one entity after another lunged from cloud and cemetery alike towards the room of unholy mist. At the center of it all was the one entity who now appeared in all his manic passion, with a rose-covered laurel upon his ovular head, his body a robe of oscillating colors that resembled the spectrum of roses Aria so dutifully marked his grave with.

The priests, struck by the power of the lording ghost, called out louder: "Fill your servants with courage to fight manfully against that reprobate dragon, lest he despise those who put their trust in you, and say with Pharaoh of old: 'I know not God, nor will I set Israel free.' Let your mighty hand cast him out of your servant, so he may no longer hold captive this person whom it pleased you to make in your image, and to redeem through your Son; who lives and reigns with you, in the unity of the Holy Spirit, God, forever and ever!"

For the first time, Donovan the spirit, caught in his own web of hubris, revealed himself to the holy men, writhed, hurtling his legion of ghouls at the two priests in vengeance. The two priests pressed on, using the sign of the cross to overpower even the greatest forces of their enemy. One by one, the legion of gray, gargoyle-like entities Donovan assembled fell at the power of their prayers.

Aria, seeing the curtain fall between Donovan's kingdom in the afterlife and the world of flesh, felt her soul sucked back into her mortal body. She sensed Donovan weakening, not just at the holy invocations, but also at the power of her will. The eternal vow had not been made. His power over her had not been fully consummated.

Still, as she watched the priests hurtle prayers and commands at him, as she watched Donovan take each blow like a great bull succumbing to the pull of the dead, she could not help but reach out to him. Donovan, almost human in his form, fled like a scared boy to the only shelter he knew in this or in any world: to Aria's embrace. Instinctively, her soul cradled his. Donovan held on far too tightly, so much so that the blue and purple returned to Aria's face and again she was almost lost to death.

Father McDonald, apparently sensing the ghost's peril, if not Aria's, called out to his peer: "By Heaven's grace, stop this, Father. This is no demon and if we continue, we'll surely risk damning our own souls to Hell. Let us call upon God to bless and cleanse him, to accept him into his holy kingdom."

Unrelentingly, Father Bernito called: "At the cost of the child? Look at her. Each moment we delay, she draws closer to death."

Unable to counter the omens written in Aria's bluish features, Father Mc-Donald joined with Father Bernito as he called out: "I command you, unclean spirit, whoever you are, along with all your minions now attacking this servant of God, by the mysteries of the incarnation, passion, resurrection, and ascension of our Lord Jesus Christ, by the descent of the Holy Spirit, by the coming of our Lord for judgment, that you tell me by some sign your name, and the day and hour of your departure. I command you, moreover, to obey me to the letter, I who am a minister of God despite my unworthiness; nor shall you be emboldened to harm in any way this creature of God, or the bystanders, or any of their possessions."

Donovan, crippled by the thought of harming this most beautiful creature of God, this Aria he so loved, weakened his grip. *I have no place,* he communicated to Aria. *I don't belong, not here, not anywhere!*

Aria, still blue, still weakened, regained the power of voice. "Stop it," she shrieked. "You're hurting him!"

The holy water descended upon her skin with flinty Latin vowels. Donovan, a mad wave of pulsing red light, let go of the one creation he swore never to let go of.

His ghostly arms, now tentacle-like, reached for Aria. She reached as well, turning bluer, purpler in her skin as she did so. Donovan, searching into her eyes with the clear blue orbs he still possessed, let go.

By Aria's mirror, a portal to what must've been Hell opened. She saw the defeated ghouls Donovan had dominated to get to her waiting with demonic arms to welcome him into their fold, to tear him to pieces for the evils he had visited upon them. At another priestly summons, Donovan lashed out, tentacle-like, smashing the mirrors, decapitating the bedposts, grabbing pictures of Wallace holding Aria, smashing them in a frantic madness.

Aria sat up, grabbing the priest with the might of the heavens, begging. "Fathers, please! He's not evil! He's just in pain!"

Wallace rushed over to cradle Aria. The violence that was in Aria pushed Wallace back, up against the hard plaster wall.

Father McDonald checked on the fallen man. Wallace shook the pain from his shoulders and ascended.

"See the cross of the Lord. Be gone, you hostile powers!" Father Bernito cried in Donovan's direction.

Aria shrieked in even greater decibels, feeling in corporeal form her ghostly husband's pain. This time everything from the old bedroom—the photos of the wedding, the necklaces snaking their away across the dresser, the lava lamp, the rings—all swirled in a supernatural fire as the wrath of Donovan feasted on the material world.

Cries of the primal, of agony, pain of flesh and spirit, roared back from reams of blood-colored flame that had consumed the far wall.

In a final moment of desire, Donovan reached his ghostly arm, fighting to take hold of the eternity he saw bottled up in the woman he loved. Her pale hand, now more human, though nearly limp, reached weakly towards her ghostly love, until the ghoul, sensing the agony he'd caused, withdrew his ghostly hand in shame. For a moment, the two loves shared every lover's dream, and every lover's nightmare: they could see each other as they truly were. Aria could see in the eyes, so supernaturally blue, the child within him. Somehow, he truly believed that hurting the corporeal would not be hurting Aria, but setting her free. Somehow, he'd forgotten his humanity. The flames gathered. Aria reached to pull Donovan back into her. Sensing her fear, the specter placed the palm of his ghostly hand upon her fleshly palm, touching like they had when they were mere babies, taking their first breaths on this earth. Their single moment, lost in each other's eyes, in the truth of their vices and their virtues, knitted them, yet pulled them even farther apart. And so, with the flames of damnation all around the ghostly form, Aria knew Donovan's true aim. She'd only be free if he were dead, forever dead. She'd only live if his hold on her were to die.

You must live! You must have your child, she could feel him saying. *I choose Hell so that you might have Heaven.*

With pain still coursing in the blue of his eyes, Donovan fell to the unyielding fire, to the delight of the very ghouls he'd once so dominated and tormented. Aria saw the gargoyle-shaped demons lunging towards him, spears ready, before the vision of Hell ceased, eaten by its own fire. Aria screamed, begging Donovan to retract, but she saw only a small, supernatural rose of fire left where Donovan once was. Donovan had joined with the flames; for her, he'd journeyed to Hell.

The priests finished their litany of prayers, thanking the Lord and blessing the house. As they did, they stepped towards the supernatural oddity on the floor. Before their hands could reach it, the rose crackled in triumphant fire. Just as quickly, the rose burst into pure white flame and was gone.

CHAPTER 23:

Coda

〜 After Aria recovered the next morning, she took to stepping on the cold, hard oak, if only to feel in the pressing of her skin against tangible matter that she was still alive.

The house will soon be gone, she thought. *This is probably the only case where the buyers might look upon an exorcism as a good thing.*

Aria, exhausted as she was, attempted to avoid any thoughts of all that would go when she moved in with Wallace after the honeymoon. She attempted to exorcise Donovan from her mind and heart just as he'd been exorcised from her home, but some exorcisms are not so easy. Aria kept walking, kept pacing, until the real thought on her mind could no longer be avoided: *The love of my life is in Hell. God, help him. God help us all.*

It was at the intersection of such thoughts that she encountered Father McDonald, minus Father Bernito, walking the house one last time himself.

"Sorry, Aria," he said. "I didn't mean to disturb you, child, especially now that you're looking a little more, well, normal. I'm just clearing up some points for my account to Rome."

"It's okay, Father. I never had a chance to thank you."

"It was Father Bernito who led the exorcism."

"But it was you who tried to talk reason, who tried to free my love without. . . banishing him."

"I've noted in my report that this was no legitimate case of demonic possession. Rome will be happy with that."

"If it wasn't possession, then what was it, Father?" Aria asked blankly.

"You already know. For such a young woman, you're wiser than the lot of us put together."

Aria turned to the window. The mists that had consumed all of Burgundy Hill were clearing, but not her confusion.

Father McDonald faltered. His wrinkles quaked and his eyes grew dark, then flashed a sad, heavenly grace.

Aria's face turned back from the yellow light gathering in the window. A single wayward rivulet cut a path down her cold cheek. "He's in Hell, Father," she said unevenly. "He went to Hell so that I might live. I have to do something. I can't live if I know he's truly died."

"Don't walk the path Donovan did, Aria," Father McDonald advised. "Learn from him. No man who sacrifices himself for love of another is without God. I went, prepared myself, to do battle with Hell. Instead, I saw a soul preparing itself for Heaven."

Aria turned to the priest disbelievingly.

"Just because I've studied at a theological university doesn't mean I'm a wise man, Aria," Father McDonald said. "God's ways are the greatest mystery this world has ever known. I don't see why God's arms would be so short as not to reach your Donovan. After what I've seen, I'd say he's taken his first step towards God."

"Are you saying you believe in ghosts, Father?"

"I'm saying," Father McDonald noted, noticeably surprised at the words on his lips, "that I believe in men."

Aria smirked, the pink returning to her lips.

"Your late husband and your fiancé both made believers of me," Father McDonald said. "I've spent my whole life in God's service, but it was they who knew Him. It was they who knew love."

Father McDonald faltered on the word, as if unable to capture its full essence. Aria caught wind of his vulnerability and marched up closer to the elderly priest.

"You sound as if you knew great love yourself," she said, studying the serenity of his face.

"I knew arrogance. I knew selfishness. Had I known that then, it might've been me walking at the side of the woman I loved." Father McDonald paused, sifting through the residue of years that had collected in his heart. "But I didn't. That's why God blessed me with the priesthood. To show me what great love truly is."

Aria looked right into the holy man's pale eyes. "She must've been remarkable, this woman," she said.

Father McDonald smirked, looking down. "She looked a lot like you, years ago," Father McDonald said. "She's just as beautiful today. You should've seen her, Aria. She never left your side until I forced her and Wallace away. She was so strong, such a sight to behold."

"I never thought I'd say this, but I want to see my mother."

Father McDonald laughed.

"I have wedding details to discuss. Would you like to come?" Aria asked.

"I'd like to walk with you a bit, if I could. I never knew the joy of having a little girl, a joy I hope you'll soon know."

Aria pecked the graying bristles on Father McDonald's cheek. "After what we've been through, I'll always think of you as a second father," she said. "You are still going to preside at my wedding, aren't you?"

"Only if this is the last one. I'm not going to live forever, Aria."

Aria laughed, then grew serious, solemn. "I disagree," she said in contemplation, staring out at the sky. "I think that's what Donovan's presence was trying to tell me me, Father, that we all live forever when we're remembered with love."

 Lying down to rest that night, Aria still feared for Donovan, despite the comfort Father McDonald gave her earlier.

I just have to know. I have to be certain he's all right, she said, listening for her heart's reply.

Though she looked outside, half-hoping to catch a glimpse of her eternal lover, Aria realized, in a moment not without cathartic value, that she had grown up. Night was dying and with it her girlish views of love. Soon the wick of dawn would ignite the clouds in a new day. The storms would pass, only to rise in new form. The ghosts of her past would be permanently exorcised. The world would be at rest, yet teeming in new life. And how much more peaceful it all looked, Burgundy Hill, the town of her birth, after Donovan's departure. The skies looked like the night of first creation. The winds felt so strong against the stubborn leaves of winter and the mists. They felt natural now, without their putrefying hue. The whole scene was a panorama of quiet grace, a reminder that this was the hour, the only hour of life that Woman ever has on this earth before she, too, must fall to time.

Gone were the days when the child Aria ran so freely about the shores. Gone were the days when she necked with boys by the tides. And gone were the days of the bride that might have been, the life that might've been, but wasn't, lost to the grave of dreams. Yet, every one of those Arias still existed deep within her, though they were tempered by the maturity she gained from her struggles, in the same way that the winds tempered the night. And so, silently, Aria reached out across her thoughts and the years she held there, touching the baby her, the girl who first touched Donovan, in a communion of ages, of epochs of life. She knew that the dream lived on, even if by dying, that a peculiar grace, a mature grace, would enlighten her features and her life.

But still, the one pressing question remained.

The night holds no answer, Aria thought, quietly resigning herself to bed.

She pulled the covers, one of the last, the only, unpacked items, over her, in the very bed where he'd possessed her nights ago. Though Aria didn't sleep—brides-to-be never do—she could feel a vision of sorts, something like a dream, but more animate, seizing her senses.

Walk with me, a bright light said, rose in color, but burning like a star.

Is it you or is it my dream? Aria asked her own thoughts.

It was the way she always felt when thinking of Donovan, when contemplating the nature of love. *Is it real or am I just dreaming? Can any two people ever be as close as we were and know each other, really know each other, through and through?*

You are love, she imagined Donovan saying. *Whatever my eternal self is, I owe to you.*

"That's the girl in me," Aria said with a smirk. "That is something I'd always wished he'd say."

And yet, she knew it to be true.

Just then, as if in confirmation of her thoughts, Aria could've sworn she saw her groom rising, more luminous than the brightest sky, his skin and hair, each a separate hue of rosy light lost in the blue of his eternal stare. How beautiful he looked, how serene. She drank him in, all of him, the pain he brought to her life, the love that he always provided as a balm.

Is it real, Aria asked herself again, *or just a dream?*

She reached out, seeking to attain the untouchable truth of love. Donovan smiled, his face almost visible in the blinding light.

You are the ghost of all seasons of love, Aria said to him. *Tell me what I need to know.*

The answer was always within you, the figure of light said, or so Aria would have it. *No man ever fully knows any woman, and yet he loves. No woman ever truly understands any man, and yet she loves. That is the mystery. That is the miracle of it all.*

Aria smiled. The words were so simple. The words were so true.

I can't be there in the flesh this Saturday, though I will be there in spirit, to hand you over one last time. Know, though, that I won't be able to come back anymore, where I'm going.

I know. I've always known, Aria replied.

So I have a favor to ask of you, the spirit of light said. *Let me have a wedding dance, in advance.*

This once, Aria knew that Donovan asked nothing more. How could he ask of her that which she so freely gave?

She felt no fear dancing with the light. And so, she imagined herself and her groom of her early life dancing, all of Heaven attendant, filled with rapturous applause.

Aria imagined that it was she and Donovan who danced together through all the years of her life, from when she was a baby to when she grew old. It was such a sweet illusion, and yet so real, this ecstasy of love. For just one more moment in eternity, she could smell him, that English Leather Musk he always wore. She could drink in the warmth of his skin, the crook between neck and shoulder where her chin found so much comfort. How much of her love was in the details, in the slight brush of her cheek against his hair, in the meeting, uniting, and dividing, of their eyes. At times, that simple comfort was better than all sex, for it achieved a unity beyond the physical, beyond the emotional, simply beyond. For the first time, in this slow dance that was something like a waltz, Aria knew that it was she who was leading, that Donovan sought not to take her power, to clip her wings and cage her to his vision of who she must be. And in her streams of thought Aria sought not to make Donovan more social, or socially acceptable for that matter, more gregarious, more dashing, or more wise. It was a dance of acceptance, a dance eternal, in which each was separate, yet the same. It was the dance they were always meant to dance in life, only this time they got the steps right.

It's time for the dance to end, isn't it? she asked the light. *It's time for me to Mrs. Aria Stevens.*

It's time for you to be who you always were, the woman I love.

Aria didn't know whether that was Donovan's reply, or her own thoughts, but she liked the line, and she knew it to be true.

Without ever truly saying her goodbyes, Aria felt herself awake, fully. While she could've played the psychoanalytical game with herself, contemplating if it was all a dream, she knew: That's all love ever is. It is the dream and the reality. It is the keeper of worlds that divides as well as unites.

He's in Heaven, she said to herself in comfort, *because he is my Heaven. Thank you, merciful God. Thank you for the gift of his life.*

When Aria saw her mother next, she realized that she was not the only one who had changed since the events of a day ago. Bella looked older, but milder, with a fresh strength of feature that gave life to her hazel eyes as she toiled away at the guests' party favors.

"Aren't there any last-minute wedding details you're going to hammer me with?" Aria asked, with a grace that could've only come from her mother.

Bella's dismissive glance stopped Aria cold. Aria watched as Bella lifted up a single hand, gracefully, and searched for words beyond her meaning.

"I'm sorry if I became the monster mother trying to manipulate everything. It's your wedding, and I'm okay with whatever you decide."

Aria nearly died of shock, though a happy shock, one she least expected.

"What I'm trying to say, Aria," Bella whispered, reaching out to her child, "is that you've been through more than I can imagine and after seeing him reach out to you, in his own destructive way, I remembered how much you loved him, how much you love him still."

"Mother."

Bella again held up her hand, a sign of a mother's strength, an admission of her weakness.

"I should've been there for you, really been there for you, after his death," Bella said. "I shoved one man after another at you, hoping you'd date, that you'd heal and move on. Some good that strategy has done me. I'm so sorry I didn't understand you."

"There's no need to apologize. You're my mother. I'm your daughter."

"If you want to talk about him, talk about the loss, I'm here for you now, as I should've been all along. We can share memories," Bella added, containing her emotion, "of husbands dead and husbands that should be."

"I'd like that—after the wedding," Aria said coyly.

"About that, dear. If you want to cancel the wedding, if you and Wallace—"

"I love Wallace. I need Wallace," Aria argued, "and I think Donovan understands that now. I think even I understand that now. Wallace was God's gift to me after Donovan's passing. He deserves a good wedding, and I intend to give him one."

Bella smiled. Her fingers fumbled tying off the plastic candy wrappers. She stopped, turned to her daughter. "When I saw you there, so limp, so pale," Bella started, choking up just a bit, "I thought of the mother I never was to you."

"Mother, stop."

"Let me finish," Bella insisted. "I always put my career first and argued that it was only for the best. I never thought of doing otherwise. I can't entirely apologize: I still believe I did what I had to do."

"You did, Mother."

"But not with the love I should have shown you. Not always with your best interests at heart. My career meant so much to me. My legacy meant so much to me. I should've realized my true legacy was you."

"You're going to make me cry, aren't you?" Aria asked. "This is all designed to give me a good cry, isn't it?"

"Donovan figured out in a second what it's taken me a lifetime to learn," Bella said, composing herself. "I love you. The napkins, the chair covers, the bridesmaids' gifts, the party favors," she gestured, pointing downward, "they all matter so little without you."

Bella took a moment, let the emotion pass over her.

"It's just that I wanted a real mother-daughter moment," she said. "I guess I wanted something that might make up for all the times I missed when you were a girl. I'm sorry I let it get the best of me."

Aria kissed Bella's cheek. "I know, Mother," she said. "I always knew."

"And now I do too." Bella battled on, saying: "That's why I'm giving you back your wedding. That's my gift to you." The old matron turned to walk out the door, but stopped, still held by that magical bond of mother and daughter. "Call me if you need help. If you don't need to call, that's fine, too."

"These candies for the guests aren't going to wrap themselves," Aria said, inviting Bella over.

As Aria tied off her first of a great many treats for the guests, Bella's fingers joined hers. Truly, Aria lacked the grace to neatly tie the little plastic chocolates.

"That's not the way you—"

"Mother?"

"Yes, Aria?"

"Don't start."

"It's just that I have experience with these, dear, and you, well, you clearly don't." Bella smirked. "You know when I first made them?" Bella waited, but Aria refused to follow up with the mandatory question. "At my bridal shower. It was my mother who helped me make them right before I had you."

"Mother."

"Dear?"

"There's something to be said for the quiet moments of life."

"I'm just trying to—"

"I know, Mother. But let's worry about the wedding first. I'm not even married yet and you're already trying to knock me up."

"I know," Bella said, clearly overjoyed. "Isn't it wonderful?"

∽ Later that night, Aria paced the cold moonlight that graced the mahogany of her bedroom suite, reconciling fear with resolution. She knew that the napkins, tablecloths—even the bows on the guests' seats—would match in a pink and white medley of color. Her mother had seen everything down to the most minute of details. Aria's question was larger than a bride concerned with the intricacies of a reception hall: She was concerned with the intricacies of her life. Even after all that she had experienced, with Wallace, with her mother, with Donovan, she still had cold feet. How could she, the perpetual widow, walk the aisle, celebrating the second best day in her life when the man she betrayed might very well still be lost, somewhere out in eternity? And was it not she who brought in the priests, the mystics, the holy men who compelled him there? How dare they! And yet, how conflicted she felt. Had not Donovan acted on his own volition, had he not ultimately chosen to leave her? How dare Donovan make so grave a choice without consulting her!

In the icy twilight, she no longer heard definitively from the ghost she forcibly expelled from his own home. That dance they shared somewhere in the land between dreams and reality truly was the last music of their shared soul. She'd never once heard whispers in the moonlight. She never felt the cool tingle of fingers along the frayed edges of her hair. His presence, forever looming, felt vanquished, as did anything even remote enough to be called feeling. It wasn't that Aria didn't love. It's just that the supernova fire of her love and her fury had managed to extinguish any ruling flame from her heart. She felt old, used up, like anything but the bride of tomorrow.

You are gone, Aria whispered, hardly believing the words she felt the need to articulate. *And I'm gone with you.*

Aria felt the essence of the world take her flesh, felt as ashen as the photos of herself and Donovan along the shores of yesteryear. How full of life the waves of the ocean were then, how full of searing fire the sands of the coast, how animated were cloud and star. Now, they were little more than a trite post-Impressionist painting gracing the firmament of the forgotten in her mind. Aria might still walk, might still breathe, might still ache, if more minutely, but that which gave her life had long ago given her death. She felt insensible to the world, as though she were but a widow to the past.

I can't marry him tomorrow, Aria finally declared.

I'm so embarrassed to say it, but I can't. She could feel the protest of love within herself. She really, truly did love Wallace, but what was that love but the coursing blood beneath the settled scar? The wound had been inflicted. Her heart would never again be made whole. *God help me,* Aria asked repeatedly, thinking of the soul she had seen, albeit briefly, condemned to fire, of the man she might condemn to ice. But the wind held no answers, and so in her old wedding bed she fitfully slept.

It was then that Aria's spectral husband stood by her, touching her momentarily so that she might be comforted. He felt the irony of it all. This was to be the day of his true wedding, the day Aria joined him in eternal union. Now, it would be the anniversary of a death in another sense; it would be his exile. Donovan had changed. He had continued to grow. Sure, he still wore the laurel of roses, but in place of his sanguine fire there was now only purest light, the multifaceted color of love in its most absolute form.

In the uncounted hours of eternity, Donovan apprenticed himself to God. After his dance of apology to Aria, his purgatory became drifting behind traveling lovers, listening to their promises, offering prayers that whatever love he felt might in some way be of use to those lovers to come. And how much he had seen: foolish boys nearly cheating on their girlfriends before love's promise, in the form of an unexpected spectral rose, whispered to their senses. And perhaps most tragically, unhappy lovers settling for unhappy marriages, who he counseled to go out, together, and reignite the spark of their love. Donovan would show them how: He advised them to look at each other as they first did, all those years ago, with eyes of love. He whispered to them to honor the whole person, past, present, future, and say I love you, not just in word, but in action. Indeed, the former ghoul had become a veritable scholar in love, and how freely he shared that wisdom and love with others, as it was meant to be shared. Now, he was complete—love in all its forms, in all its seasons.

And so, Donovan drifted until he could not keep his thoughts from Aria. He had to feel the painful sweetness of comforting her before the day of his departure. Before he could ascend, before he could truly leave, he felt the light in her room still calling to him. Already sensing his time was up, Donovan descended to cradle his baby doll one last time. Donovan could picture only too well what Aria would look like in her wedding dress tomorrow. He still gripped, with a fierceness reserved for the undead, that one pleasant memory of Aria time could never take away: an elegant, stray chestnut lock catching a splinter of afternoon sunlight as she marched up, standing opposite the aisle, on no man's arm but his own. He'd never had a son, would never see her holding his baby—but this one memory he'd have forever.

Despite all the pain he felt for having become the embodiment of their love, Donovan wanted to picture Aria eternally in that first primordial moment of love against which all other loves are measured. For all her faults and all her emotional infidelities, was she still not that beautiful creature born to love—to be loved? Surely, God did not create her to punish one wayward soul. For all the pain she brought the ghost of her first husband, she brought so much more joy to the world, as she'd bring to Wallace, as she'd bring to her future sons and daughters.

Before leaving, Donovan wanted to express his appreciation, his sorrow, for all that she was, for all that he became. If his soul could be made into words, he knew what it'd say. And so he, in painful gentility, stroked Aria's hair, but his mind kept trying to pass on to her that which language could not contain. He openly wondered: How majestic, this creature called woman, this glory of all creation. In form and grace, how like the poetry of Heaven; in her endless capacity to feel, how like God. There she slept in one of her daughters, the beauty of the world—life's beginning, its greatest mystery, the ark through whom all come, mother and child. How Donovan longed to unravel her every wonder, her every thought. How he longed to be eternally united. And yet, how impossible this hope was, for how separate Man and Woman were, even when the same—and how much he felt this, the paradox of creation, how much he felt every man's pain. Never was Man to understand this delicate enigma, no matter how close he might come. Too complex was she, too unfathomable, too capricious and too wise. Even as he ascended, at long last letting his baby go, Donovan knew the eternal truth of it: Earth had no greater mystery than the depths of a woman's heart. But how he thanked God for this mystery most divine—for Heaven held no greater glory than to be held in the strength of her arms.

CHAPTER 24:

A New Movement Begins

꩜ Aria could see Donovan in these moments, in these small flashes of goodness, of love, of brilliant virtue. He had been a ghostly murderer, a monstrosity trying to take her life, to remove her from this world, even if in a distortion of what he wrongly appraised as love. Donovan had committed, so nearly, the greatest of all sins. But to Aria, the man was more than the sum of his sins. He was those moments the light caught hold and held the treasure that was his bluest of eyes. He was the laugh that rolled through all clouds, demolishing all but their silver lining that eventually gave birth to only sun. Donovan was his moment of maximum virtue. He was more than the greatest of his flaws. He was protector, sinner, man. He was human. Fully human, even after he was dead. That is how Aria cared to remember him, to keep him alive. She remembered something of what she felt to be his words of last night: *I experience God through you.* That is how he lived. That is how she hoped Donovan would keep her alive as well.

I forgive you, she whispered, saying the three most painfully beautiful words she had uttered in her whole life. *And I love you. To love is to forgive, and to forgive is to love.*

And she meant it. She loved not her fanciful dream, her idealized version from her youngest days of some boy holding a pearl on the distant shores of time, but the full man, in all his triumphs, in all his failings. Just as Aria sensed he now loved her, the full woman, as she always was, even when changing, as she always would be.

I need your strength, she whispered adamantly, adjusting the lace on her dress. *Walk me down the aisle—one last time.*

She could feel the back of her dress lace up, could almost smell the scent of a thousand roses. They seized her, gently, if only to let go, like a flurry of spring breezes grown silent at the season's change.

Aria took a breath, savoring it, then began woman's eternal march down the aisle that would ultimately lead to the rest of life. Down the rose-strewn carpet she stepped, serenaded by Pachebel's Canon in that merciful union called marriage. At each sonorous step, she could feel Donovan at her side, on her arm, taking the role of the father she lost so long ago. It was more than apology; it was his letting go. Straight into the years they marched, towards the man who'd give Aria her baby, who'd be there through the strain of everything from diaper duty to paying for college, who'd help her go back to school and get the MBA that'd lead her to be a company vice president before she retired, who'd hold her hand the very moment she passed from the world. Aria could sense Donovan showing her all of this not in anger, but in offering.

They'd never really said goodbye; lovers never really do. So they savored each other's presence, silently, in reverence, in awe at the painful beauty that was, not Man, not Woman, but this stranger entity, Man and Woman, together.

Aria knew that Donovan would be there right up until he guided Wallace's hand onto her own. Then her heart sensed he'd disappear into the eternity that awaited her, that he'd be gone, that only Mrs. Aria Stevens would remain.

And so it was that the moment Aria ended her march, looking into the eyes of the man who'd be the father of her children, the moment their two hands touched for the first time as husband and wife, her eyes were full of only this heavenly mystery called love.

And yet, in the traces of the deepest corners of the woman's heart, a place unattainable to the world and its men, Aria could almost swear she felt Donovan still watching from some farther cliff overlooking the temporal tides, calling back, in the faint echoes of eternity, to see that she was okay.